GAMBLER'S GIRL

GAMBLER'S GIRL

JOHN TANNER

CUTTING EDGE

ISBN-13: 978-1-957868-35-6

Published by
Cutting Edge Books
PO Box 8212
Calabasas, CA 91372
www.cuttingedgebooks.com

CHAPTER ONE

J ohnny Blaise fired his six-shooter into the ceiling and let out a rip-roaring yell. He patted the rainbow garter of Molly Bryan in the Triple Nugget Saloon in Dodge City. Then he measured her bosom with his eye.

"Ten bucks says Molly's got the swellest garter in town, and twenty that her tits beat anything you can see from here to San Antonio." The luscious blonde arched her large breasts confidently and stared contemptuously at the Mexican's sharp, pointed bosom.

"Wait a minute Johnny," the bartender begged. "No shooting please or Bat Masterson will have my license. I don't care if you strip the girls and hold a beauty contest. But for God's cakes, don't fire that."

"What the hell happened to Wyatt Earp?" Johnny asked. "Ain't he marshall? When Wyatt was here you could shoot anything."

"Wyatt's gone to Tombstone," the man told him. "Bat's a tough hombre. So please stop the shooting." He turned to Buck Ranston. "You willing to take the man's bet?"

Buck took the money and gave it to the bartender with some of his own. Then he pulled Olive Gomez' knee up on the dark bar. By stretching her long, shapely leg, the pretty Mexican girl just made the top of the wood counter. She strained to keep her leg upright while the judges surveyed her coffee-colored skin above the stocking line and the violet garter. The men seemed to be taking a terribly long time about it. Several times the girl had to lower her leg and put it back up. Finally, they fingered her garter carefully, lifted it and snapped it hard against the girl's skin. She winced, and the men laughed.

"Just wanted to make sure it was yours honey," Buck said. "Dodge City is getting full of girls who wear false titties and a lot more." Johnny weaved a little drunkenly around Buck's girl. "Want to bet my girls figure is better? Twenty bucks."

"Why the hell not?" Buck said joyfully. They were in a gay, rollicking mood, an end of the trail mood that made them feel lightheaded and ready for anything. "Take off your duds Olive."

The Mexican girl removed her dress and stood exposed in her frilly underdrawers. She wore no bust guards and her firm, pointed breasts jutted out defiantly.

The men looked on impressed.

"Now you," Johnny said with all the dignity he could muster. He winked at Buck as Molly removed her clothes. Her large, mature breasts made Olive's look like a little girl of promise. Her full hips and robust thighs clad in a flimsy pair of undergarments similarly made the sleek Mexican girl far less sexy. The men's eyes told one another that while the Mexican was beautiful and electric in her sex-appeal, she could not stand beside this blonde goddess with the strapping white thighs and globe-like breasts.

Buck took one look at Olive's tight-lipped angry mouth and realized that she would be deeply hurt by any contest involving the girl's total measurements. He made a quick decision.

"Listen, I don't want to spend too much money betting," he cried. "Let's stick to garters for now okay. So we'll have all the money we need to play cards, buy liquor and keep the girls happy. Let's get back to the garters, boys. What do you say?"

He winked at Johnny and snapped the colorful garters on both girl's thighs. Olive gave an involuntary groan as one man, quite drunk, stretched the garter taut and then let go. The girls put their dresses on without looking at one another.

Finally the judges huddled and spoke in low tones.

"I'm getting tired of keeping my leg up like that," Molly said, her blue Irish eyes flashing angrily. "Damn it, you all make me feel like a cow at a county fair. What the hell did I get into this for in the first place. Hell I could be doing myself good upstairs."

Johnny laughed drunkenly and patted his pocket. "Don't worry Molly. I'll make it up to you."

"You'll come upstairs with me?" she said hopefully. "Why not?" Johnny Blaise said good-naturedly. "We're here to have a good time, ain't we?"

"Damn right," Buck seconded him. "One thing I insist on. After a long drive's over, we want to kick up our heels. I'll even take Senorita Gomez upstairs. We'll get some bottles and have us the biggest damn party in Dodge City."

"Not her," Molly spat out. "She don't work here. She works at the Golden Burro at the other end of town. She's just visiting. You ain't going to take that girl upstairs."

"The Mexican girls wins," the bartender said. "On account of the garter not only looks wonderful but it's perfumed wonderful."

Buck let out a rebel yell and lifted the slim, beautiful girl off the floor.

"Come on kid. You and me's got to celebrate. Where can we go?"

"Come with me Querido," she said soothingly, staring coldly at the other girl. "And you Senor," she said to Johnny. "If you want action you come to the Golden Burro. That is if that one leaves you any money upstairs."

Johnny laughed. He lifted out a fat wad of greenbacks. "Hell don't worry. I got money. And there's plenty more where that came from. About thirty thousand. Just on my ranch alone. If I add to the one my brother Tom owns next door, why girl you got a new state practically."

He shot drunkenly into the ceiling again and let out a war whoop.

"Please mister," the bartender begged. "I don't want no trouble with the Marshall. He's trying to stop the gunplay while General Sherman's in town. He don't want any martial law here. The federal government's threatened to do it twice. All they need is an order from Sherman."

"You mean Uncle Billy himself'll be here?" Johnny said surprised. "I'm surprised he'd show his face here with so many ex-Johnny Rebs around. Lot of people don't like him round here. I'm sure of that."

"My boss don't like him," Olive spat contemptuously. "She comes from Georgia where he burned everything. The way she talks she like to kill him with her bare hands. He better not come near the Golden Burro!"

"Listen Olive," the bartender said nervously, "you'd better stop that talk. Masterson's looking around for malcontents who might start trouble. You'll get Lola in big trouble shooting your mouth like that."

"Say what's this Golden Burro like? Buck asked curiously. "That must have opened since we were here last. Got good looking girls there Olive?"

The Mexican smiled, flashing her even white teeth.

"Oh yes, yes. Wonderful girls. Beautiful figures. And they are much more fun than what they have here."

Buck winked. "Better than the girls they got below the deadline?" The deadline was the limit of the red light district where the whores unabashedly carried on their trade in special cribs.

"How you try compare crib girls with Lola's girls?" Olive Gomez said indignantly. "Our girls have real class. They use beautiful perfume, they know about food and wines and cards and they can make a man happy in every way."

"Not," she said contemptuously, looking pointedly at the blonde girl, "by taking off their clothes and showing their big fat bodies."

The men saw Molly bridle as Olive continued.

"Watch your dirty mouth you greaser!" Molly said. "Just because you're flat-chested don't talk down anybody else."

"Me flat?" Olive said venomously. "You must be blind. I am built better than you. In Juarez the rancheros used to fight to sleep with me. One night with Olive used to be worth an all day ride on a horse into town. They hired a painter to make nude picture of me for their wall. Don't call me flat, you fat pig from Nebraska."

Molly came close to her and slapped her face hard. For a moment the Mexican was so stunned, she stood there speechlessly. Then she reacted by slapping the other girl even harder.

"Bitch, tub of lard, pig woman, fat belly. The only kind of man who would pick you is one who wanted a mattress! You are ugly, ugly, ugly!" Olive screamed.

"Hey wait a minute girls," Johnny said laughing. The fight was an extra dividend to the end-of-the-trail celebration. He slapped his thigh with glee as the girls continued to insult each other shrilly.

"Stop them," the bartender said. "You can hear the squalling down to the Sheriff's office. Come on girls. Stop it!"

The two combatants ignored them as they hurled curses at one another. Their faces were red with anger and their bosoms rose and fell rapidly as they continued to scream at the top of their lungs. When Johnny and Buck tried to pull them away from each other, they pushed them back, determined to be as profane as possible.

"Come on ladies!" Johnny said. "This ain't no time for that."

Suddenly Molly lunged for Olive and angrily knocked her to the floor. In a thrice, the two girls were a mass of tangled legs scissoring the air, their skirts flying above their strong legs and thighs. As they fought, scratched and pulled, their caterwauling continued at high pitch.

Buck and Johnny admired the girls' legs and lacy drawers as they pulled at each others' hair and screamed curses.

The two cowboys and the bartender watched helplessly as the girls continued their fight. The bartender tried vainly to pull them apart but succeeded only in being knocked severely against the bar.

Olive, her fiery Mexican anger inflamed now, tore at the other girl's dress until it was split down the middle. Then she removed the girl's bust guards and threw them out. Then she bit the blonde girl's neck. Molly let out a blood-curdling yell.

"Hey what's going on there," a voice behind them demanded. The two cowboys turned to see a tall, dapper young man in a immaculate gray frock coat and trousers with a gold-headed cane in his hand.

"Just a little squabble between two girlies," Buck said affably, a little amused by the tenderfoot's elaborate regalia.

"Get up you two," the dapper man ordered. "Get up at once, damn it!"

The girls paid no heed. They were too heavily embroiled in their private fight to look up.

"Now look stranger," Johnny said politely. "Stay out of this. It ain't none of your business. Unless you want to get what happened to him," He pointed to bartender who lay unconscious against the bar.

"It's my business to stop that fight," the newcomer said evenly. "I'll count three," he said in a louder voice. "And then you'll get up or I'll jail you both."

"Say who the hell do you think you are?" Johnny said angrily. "Going around threatening people." He moved his hand toward his holster.

"You move that hand another inch," said the stranger coolly "and you'll be jailed too."

The Mexican pushed the blonde away from her at that moment and stood up uncertainly. Johnny helped Molly to her feet.

"Mr. Masterson," she said. "I'm sorry. She started it."

Johnny Blaise's eyes widened. "You're Bat Masterson? The Bat Masterson? Marshall here?"

"That's right," the newcomer said, smiling.

Johnny put out his hand. "Well pardon me for interfering with an officer in pursuit of his duty. And I'm sure glad to meet you."

Bat Masterson shook hands with both of them, and sighed.

"Normally I don't spend much time breaking up dogfights between the girls here. But I thought for a minute murder was being committed."

"You were right," Molly said, feeling her throat and wincing." Let's go to your hotel Johnny. As far from here as possible. She's not human. She's a vampire."

"Idiota!" Olive spat. "Come amigo, we go to the Burro."

"Can I buy you a drink sometime Bat?" Johnny said as he turned to leave with Molly.

"Sure. Like that very much. I'd like to talk about Texas with you. One of my favorite places. What's your name by the way?"

"Johnny Blaise. This is Buck Ranston. Just finished driving up a herd from the Rio Grande."

"Blaise," Masterson said, his face lighting up. "You got a brother named Tom? Big guy with dark hair?"

"That's him. You know Tom?"

"Know him? Listen, get him to tell you about the wild time we had in Juarez, Mexico about three years ago. We practically turned the town on it's ear. That man can put whiskey away."

"That's Tom all right," Buck said proudly.

"How come he's not with you?" Bat said.

"Well, he don't like Kansas much," Johnny said. "He comes up once in a while. But he prefers Mexico. He'll jump the border at the drop of a hat. Besides we got twin ranches and he's watching over both of them while I drive the cows up here."

"If you're coming," Molly said annoyed, "Come. I have to get this dress sewed up, and I'll need needle and thread."

"Got them both honey," Johnny said affably. He shook hands with Bat Masterson, waved to Buck and set off toward the Greene Hotel with Molly.

A few moments later in the upstairs bedroom at the Greene Hotel, Johnny kissed the pouting lips of Molly Bryan.

"I'd like to kill the dirty greaser," she said, still smouldering over the fight. "I can't stand any of the sluts who work in Lola's place. And she hates everyone."

"Hey simmer down honey," Johnny said, offering a freshly-opened bottle of whiskey. He took a bill from his pocket and stuffed it in the girl's torn bodice. "Tell you what, Molly. I still think you're garter was pretty and that you're better in every department. Take that ten."

Molly smiled for the first time and began to disrobe. Johnny watched her free her full-breasted voluptuous figure from the torn dress and whistled softly. The sight of the curvacious girl with her long hair falling over her naked shoulders pleased him.

"My big brother Tom should see you now honey. He'd be mighty sorry he missed Dodge this trip. Come here." He took her in his arms, crushing her firm breasts against his chest and began kissing her neck.

"You like me Johnny, really?" Molly asked coquettishly, kissing him and tickling his neck.

"Sure I do," he lied. She was beginning to bore him. He had hoped that Dodge would provide something strikingly pretty and new.

"What's the Golden Burro like," he said slowly.

"Hell you don't want to go there," she said bitterly. "It's a hangout for cheap gamblers, criminals and people hiding from the police."

"What kind of criminals?"

Molly pursed her lips. "Remember that Quantrill gang? The ones who wore Confederate uniforms and burned and looted on the Kansas broder? The South repudiated them but they went on killing anyway, pretending they were just anti-Yankee. Many of them are still around here."

"She mixes with bastards like that?" Johnny said astonished. "How come the federals don't put a stop to it?"

"They can't prove anything," Molly said. "They use different names now since Quantrill was killed. But I heard lots of stories about them and Lola. A lot of local people would like to keep General Sherman out of here because of the Quantrill men. He's in serious danger. These men would love to kill him."

"I don't like murder," Johnny said slowly. "You think Lola's involved in this, too?"

"Why not? She's a Southern fanatic." Molly's eyes were angry. Johnny kissed her and smiled.

"Let's forget Lola for a while. We got better things to do honey. You're a sight for sore eyes. Come over here."

Molly giggled as his fingers tickled her. She kissed him greedily and held him tightly to her.

"You're wonderful honey," Johnny whispered nuzzling her white skin and inhaling the smell of cologne. "You're like coming into heaven after a drive through hell."

He meant it too. The long drive from Texas was no picnic. Herding 25,000 cattle across the hot plains for a month was sheer hell. You were in the saddle twelve to eighteen hours a day and when it rained you slept soaked to the skin. Meanwhile you had to settle the inevitable disputes that arose among the small group of men who made the trip with you. It was go, go, go all the time with almost no rest. By the time they got to the railhead at Dodge City where they shipped the cattle East they felt inhuman. All of them had straggly beards and parched skins and they had been breathing dust so long they felt filled with it.

It was a rough trek and yet he would not give it up for all the world. And he could never understand his brother Tom who cheerfully gave his own herds over to him to be driven north. Tom only made the trip about once every two years.

"Oh I like the trek okay," was how his older brother put it, "but I don't care if I never go back to those cow towns. They're just cowboy traps. They want your bankroll and they'll get it if they have to show everything they got under those clothes or rig the cards.

Well the hell with 'em. If I want a bender, I'll just ride south into Juarez over the border and live it up there. You can have the Dodge Cities and Abilenes. I'll be glad to pay you anytime to drive my critters up with yours."

Johnny Blaise couldn't understand Tom. It was the cow-towns that made everything worth while. He loved the giddy noise and excitement of the places. The hub-bub of Eastern traders, women in bright new dresses, the new faces, the color of the frontier town after the endless hot drabness of the plains delighted him. And like most of the cowboys who rode with him, he couldn't wait to see the end of the trail.

All along they had been dreaming of the way it would be when they hit Dodge City. The enormous quantities of whiskey they would drink, the huge steaks they would eat and the women they would love. The women were on their minds all the time. Sitting around the campfire at night, they would tell stories of the girls they had known in Abilene and Coffeyville and Dodge City. Or in Tombstone, Virginia City or El Paso. Wherever there was a town in the West there were dance halls and whorehouses and the stories that were swapped about the girls in those towns were endless. Some of the yarns were about the amorous prowess of notorious women like Big Nosed Kate or Belle Starr. Others were about the pretty girls who had embraced scores of their friends and were still waiting at the end of the trail like a pot of gold at the end of the rainbow.

"What are you thinking about sweetie?" Molly asked her lover as they lay there together. "I hope it ain't about that greaser Olive."

"I was thinking about rainbows," Johnny Blaise said, smiling. He kissed her greedily and spanked her behind good-naturedly. "You're getting fat Molly. Too much lard back there. You ought to mount a horse more often. Riding hardens you up there."

Molly stood up miffed and ran her hands over her derriere.

"It ain't fat Johnny," she said in a hurt voice. "Every cowboy who comes into this town would like to be in your shoes. Why they look right through me like I was dressed in glass whenever I walk down the street. I got the best figure in town."

He laughed, but he was not listening too closely. A burst of male laughter from the street below followed by a series of rebel yells had drawn his attention. He rose and walked to the window to see what all the commotion was about, completely oblivious to the fact that he was wearing almost nothing.

Down below in the late afternoon sun he saw the most beautiful girl he had ever seen. A dark-haired girl with long black tresses that fell to her shoulders. Her face was strikingly beautiful and her figure, even in the sedate blue dress that covered nearly every inch of her, seemed fabulous. She seemed like a vision in that dusty Dodge City street as she walked past the post-office and blacksmith shop, almost like the visions that appeared to him on the long hot days when he lay on the ground to rest a moment between the endless chores of the trail.

He could understand the looks on the faces of the men staring at her as she passed. She was not only beautiful, she seemed completely foreign. The dress was obviously made by an Eastern dressmaker. He had seen enough sketches and even photographs to recognize the cut and he was reminded of the visit he had made to New England with their father when he was a boy. He and Tom had marveled at the beautifully dressed men and women they saw in New York and Boston and Baltimore. He remembered they had worn dresses like that.

Suddenly he knew he would have to meet her. Even if she was the highest paid girl in town. It didn't matter. He had to have her.

One night with a girl like that would make the whole trip worth while, and he could look forward to coming back soon. If the girl was as good as she looked he might even be persuaded to stay longer. He wondered what she looked like with the dress off and conjured up pictures of her magnificent white bosom and legs. She was probably as beautiful as some of the nudes he had seen in the museum in New York he thought. Beautiful white skin all over and full of a fiery passion.

"What are you staring at Johnny?" the girl in bed said plaintively. "Come back. I'm getting chilled."

"Who's that girl down there?" he said. "Near the newspaper office." The sight of the girl's proud strut had arrested his eye. Everything about her was thoroughbred. He could see that. She walked like an aristocrat among the waddling housewives, glum-looking Indians and half-drunken cowboys. Once, as she stared directly up at him, he blushed. He had never seen anyone so beautiful.

"What girl?" Molly said annoyed.

"Down there now," he said, studying the girl carefully. "Careful, boy," he told himself, "or you'll fall in love at first sight again." His brother Tom was always warning him about that, but it never did any good. All he needed was one good look at a girl that caught his eye and he was hooked. Especially when she looked and walked like a queen.

"What the hell are you looking at," Molly said at his elbow. "Oh, her. That's Penny Flynn, sister of the woman who owns the Golden Burro."

For a moment, he felt a sharp intake of breath as Penny's beautiful eyes fastened directly at his. It was almost as if she were looking at him, though he knew she could not see him.

"She new in town?" Johnny said curiously.

"Yes," Molly said disdainfully. "She's probably trying to see if her sister's in her room. Get away from there please."

"Where's the Golden Burro?" he asked. He knew he would have to meet her.

"Why?" Molly said ominously. "Ain't I good enough for you?"

"Sure you are, honey," he said slapping her rear. "But I want to meet Buck later."

"Down near the river. That big white fancy building with two stories."

"Tell me a little about Lola. I ain't caught up on the local news."

Molly shrugged. "I don't know what to tell you. She came to Dodge about six months ago with a lot of money and built that place."

"Tell me more about Lola," Johnny said. "Where'd she get the money for the Burro?"

"You sure you ain't asking because you want to sleep with her sister? Molly asked shrewdly. "I saw the way you were eying her. Like you couldn't wait to get the clothes off her back."

"Naw, you got me wrong. I just want the gossip that's all. I been on the trail a long time honey."

Molly looked dubious. "Well Lola supposedly was an actress back East. They say she met a big cattleman there not long ago and he promised to marry her. The wedding was all set, guests and big shots all invited, announcements made, when the critter lit out. Lola was the laughing stock of the town. She was madder than hell, especially since she had just lost a good part and she came out after him. First she nearly caught him in Chicago, then in Denver.

"Somehow she got him to go through with the marriage there and then the funny part happened."

"What funny part?" Johnny asked. He had hoped Molly would talk about Lola's sister too.

"Well about a week after the wedding, there was an accident on their ranch. Lola told folks he was out hunting and got hit by another hunter. It didn't go too well in Denver, that story. A lot of people cut her dead. They just refused to have anything to do with her. The way I heard it from a Denver wrangler who came through here people thought she shot him herself in revenge for jilting her back East. Anyway she sold their ranch and came out here. Then she set up the Golden Burro. She started it as a kind of show place with gambling on the side, but the best entertainment they have now goes on in the bedrooms upstairs, if you know what I mean?"

"Sure but what about her sister?" Johnny asked curiously. "Her sister one of the whores?"

He had heard of everything but not that. Still this was Dodge City, where anything could happen. Where a girl might even use her sister that way.

"I don't know what goes on in that place," Molly said irritably. "All I know is it's a trap for cowboys who come up here. I never heard of anyone going in there who didn't lose everything he had. Listen you ain't thinking of going in there Johnny are you? You're crazy if you do. Especially after you told that little Mexican you own thirty thousand dollars? Why they'd be after you with all they have. You stay here with me."

Johnny Blaise grinned and embraced the Irish girl. There was no sense in getting Molly sore. Molly was a good enough sort and she certainly made Dodge City a warmer place. But he couldn't forget the other girl. Something about her face brought her back every other minute.

"Let's have some more of this Texas Tanglefoot," he said holding up the half empty bottle of whiskey. When she was asleep would be time enough to explore the possibilities of the Golden Burro.

It didn't take too long. Two more hearty swigs of the raw whiskey and she was rocky. A third and she was hugging the pillow drowsily and repeating his name in a blurred voice. He laughed good-naturedly as he watched her snore and placed a folded ten dollar bill on her exposed rear. Then he dressed quickly and left the room.

On the way out he ran head into a tall swarthy stranger in a dark wool suit who glared at him angrily.

"Watch where you're headed cowboy!" the stranger growled adjusting the white broad-brimmed hat that had been turned askew by the collision. Whiskey from the bottle Johnny was carrying had stained his beautifully cut jacket.

"Sorry mister," Johnny said good-naturedly. "Guess I'm a little unsteady. I didn't see a thing as I came round the bend."

"Ah you wranglers are always drunk," the other man groused. "Coming down those stairs like a locomotive."

Johnny stared coolly at the tall stranger.

"I told you I was sorry didn't I?"

"Yeah I heard you," the man cried irritably. "Look what the hell you've done to my suit. I brought that all the way from Chicago damn it."

"I'll be glad to buy you another one mister if that's all that's bothering you," Johnny said politely.

The other men threw him a contemptuous glance.

"Where the hell do you think I could buy anything like that in Dodge City? Oh the hell with it. I'm wasting time talking to you. What does a cowboy know about clothes?"

"I don't like your tone mister," Johnny said softly. "I wouldn't push my luck too far if I was you. Down in Texas when a polite argument gets out of hand we don't fancy using words to settle things."

"What are you trying to do cowboy? Frighten me?" the big man said with a sneer. He moved his hand slowly to his gun and Johnny did the same. They stared at each other cautiously for a moment, waiting for each other's next move. They were interrupted suddenly by the innkeeper who ran up terrified and demonstrated with them.

J O H N   T A N N E R

"Please gents, no shooting in here. I just laid down a new rug brought all the way from New York."

"Relax Amos," the big man said smiling glacially. "Nobody's going to stain your rug." He turned his back coldly on the young cowboy, "I was just explaining something about being afraid that's all. I sort of think our young friend here understands me."

"Thank you Mr. Billings," the stocky bald-headed hotel owner said with relief. "I sent a bottle of whiskey to your room like you wanted."

The hotel man turned anxiously to Johnny.

"I was afraid you'd try to draw on Mr. Billings, son. I wouldn't do that if I was you. He was one of the best shots in Lee's army and he keeps in practice. I've seen ten men try to draw on Mr. Billings. Ain't a single one of them that got up off the ground afterwards."

"Well thanks for the news report Amos," Johnny said casually. "But maybe I'd have changed his average. You came up just as my trigger finger was getting itchy. Who is that bag of wind and what's he doing in Dodge City?"

"Well he's a lawyer from Chicago. The Santa Fe sent him up here to check into some land deals. I understand he's a pretty important man back in Illinois."

"Well he won't be important long if he tries that tone on me around here too often. I don't take kindly to that kind of talk. Never have in fact."

The hotel man shrugged. "Probably never see him. He practically lives over at the Golden Burro. He's very chummy with the owner there—Lola."

The name of the gambling place brought Johnny's smile back. "Hey, that's where I'm going Amos. Just point me right to it will you."

The hotel man pointed toward a two story frame building about 1,000 yards away.

The Texan straightened his hat, took a hearty swig of the whiskey and then tossed the empty bottle out the open doorway. Without a second's hesitation he fired a bullet at it and caught it neatly ten feet above the ground. The two men heard a high pitched scream as the bottle smashed against the hitching post near the hotel.

As they turned to see who the screamer was, they saw a beautiful young girl race past them to the far end of the lobby and hide behind a thick column.

Johnny's eyes widened as he recognized the newcomer. It was the same girl he had admired from the window upstairs. The sister of Lola Flynn, owner of the Golden Burro. He turned to apologize a moment later and stared into the angriest and most beautiful feminine eyes he had ever seen.

"I'm mighty sorry ma'am," Johnny said as he removed his hat. "It was just a game. I meant no harm."

"No, that's exactly the trouble," she stormed in a New England accent that made him smile despite himself. "You never mean any harm. You cowboys go around shooting bottles and windows in the street in a wild drunken spree and God help any poor soul who gets in your way. You're all insane children. Why, in Boston they'd have you all put away for this."

Johnny smiled. "That a fact ma'am? You come from Boston?"

"Oh you're hopeless," she wailed and ran past him up the stairs.

Johnny stared at her and his grin grew wider. Lola's kid sister had the most fascinating rear he had ever seen. It was sashaying up the stairs like a locomotive with a drunken engineer in the cab. He felt a wild impulse to rush after her and derail her into his arms.

CHAPTER TWO

The innkeeper watched Johnny nervously. The cowboy seemed poised to chase the girl up the stairs.

"You ain't aiming to cause trouble, son, are you?" he said plaintively.

Johnny laughed. "Hell, no. I'll admit I'd like to get my hands on that girl, Amos, but I guess I can wait till I see her at the Burro. Besides, I don't suppose you like the girls to take men to their rooms."

"No, sir," Amos said, looking at the doorway. "And please don't speak that way in front of my wife. She's been after me about that." He winked at Johnny and smiled.

Johnny broke out into loud guffaws. "Why, you old reprobate. You mean you're running a parlour house right here on the premises?"

"No, no, but I can't keep track of the way the guests act. You were up there with a girl yourself, weren't you?"

Johnny winked and shrugged his shoulders.

"There's a whole line of houses full of Mexican and Indian girls down a ways," Amos said helpfully. "Course, they don't compare with what they have in the Golden Burro. But believe me, son, it'll cost you much less in the end."

Johnny nodded. "Well, I'll take a look, Amos. I'm in a celebrating mood. But I don't think I'll find anything like that girlie who went upstairs. What's she charge anyway? She ain't one of them hundred dollar girls I hope. I heard Dodge City had one of those. If she is, she's still worth it."

The Texan grinned drunkenly at the hotel owner who started to reply then changed his mind and moved behind the counter. At the same moment Johnny saw a big imperious woman in a dark-hued gingham dress enter the hotel.

"Mr. Blaise," Amos said in a squeaky, frightened voice, as if he feared what Johnny might say next. "This is my wife."

Barely acknowledging the presence of the lanky cowboy in his dowdy nankeen trousers, Mrs. Greene turned her full, majestic wrath on her husband.

"Amos. Unless these Texas cowhands stop shooting up the town on their drunken sprees I'm going to sell this place and move back to Grand Island, Nebraska. It's so bad a lady can't walk through the Plaza without some foul-mouthed cowboy making remarks about her bustle. Do you know one of those men had the crust to offer me two dollars to go into a tent with him."

Johnny did not wait to hear more. He exited quickly as another volley of gunfire drowned out Mrs. Greene's words. Outside a mob of drunken cowboys, bullwhackers and mule skinners were shooting wildly at empty cans, hitchracks and stones thrown high in the dust-filled air.

"Johnny Blaise," he heard a delighted voice say behind him. "Johnny Blaise. It's me, Jake Harkins. You're just in time. We're going to hit the line. Come on along."

He recognized a burly bullwacker from Texas who regularly came up to Dodge and often stopped for a night at either his ranch or his brother's. Jake Harkins was a big good-natured man who had only three interests outside of his oxen: drinking raw whiskey, making love to wild women and playing poker. He loved Dodge City because it was a place you could combine all three twenty-fours a day, seven days a week.

"Come on Johnny," the brawny Texan insisted, wiping traces of whiskey from his grizzled beard. "I hear they got a new load of girls including a Frenchie."

"Thanks Jake," Johnny said, "but I'm kind of tired. I just been with a girl. I was just going over to a place for a sandwich and some beer."

"The hell you are," Jake said in mock anger. "The first time I see you in four months and you're turning me down."

He pulled out a buckskin sack from his shirt and held it up. "I got enough here to stake us to every girl in the line. And we can have all the beer and sandwiches you can eat in between. Come on now before I get mad."

"Aw Jake," Johnny said. "Let's make it tomorrow."

"Tomorrow," Jake roared. "Tomorrow! Hell son tomorrow I may be begging for drinks on Front street. Let's get it while the getting's good and I can pay for it. What the hell did you have on the trail—a squaw or something? Most of the wranglers and cowboys I've met went to the line before they had breakfast. Nobody knows how long the girls'll be there. You come on now or I'll tell Tom his kid brother's going soft and is spending his time laying on calico sheets up in Greene's hotel."

Johnny blushed. "Okay, okay, I'll come." He could not stand being kidded by Tom, and it was a certainty that Jake Harkins would blab the whole story in a distorted fashion as soon as he got back. He would be in for a endless teasing at the hands of his older brother whether he visited the whorehouses with the cowboys or not. He might as well go to shut Jake up.

"Good," Jake yelled. "Let's go." He introduced Johnny to the others as they walked past the numerous saloons on the main street. They were all men who had just come in with herds of cattle and were out to paint Dodge red before going back home.

As they walked down the dusty street toward the "line" the cowboys took turns shooting at cans, trying to keep them in the air and following each other's hits or misses with loud curses. When an occasional woman passed by on the wooden boardwalk that skirted the rows of buildings, they would stop. As soon as she was safely out of earshot, the oaths would resume.

For several hundred yards they continued past saloons stopping every so often to refresh themselves. By the time they reached the "line" all of them were staggering and missing the cans by a foot or more.

The "line" was a row of white shacks with red lamps outside to indicate the nature of the business inside. The shacks, fairly flimsy structures were placed far enough from the main thoroughfare so that respectable women would not be disturbed by them.

When they reach the line of brothels Johnny was surprised to see the number of waiting cowboys, wranglers, mule skinners, freighters and even tenderfeet in natty civilian clothes. The biggest group waited outside a shack toward the end of the row. Jake Harkins became immediately curious about the shack and made a bee-line for it with the others following.

They passed groups of cowboys waiting good-naturedly in the darkness. The waiters were keeping their spirits high by passing bottles of whiskey from hand to hand, singing popular trail songs, including some that were unprintable. At intervals one of the cowboys would restlessly fire his six shooter into the air and give a rebel yell.

"What the hell is going on inside?" Jake Harkins asked one of the knot of cowboys around the most popular shack. "Who in hell's name is in there, the Queen of Sheba? She must be pretty good to get a bunch like this around here."

"It's a French girl who came up here from Mexico," one of the men confided. "She's built so lovely you can't hardly breathe when she's next to you. And every time she moves, well her bosom heaves like there's an earthquake, if you know what I mean."

"Sure," another waiter admitted. "But her rates are kind of high and she keeps raising them everytime the crowd out here gets bigger. The girls in the other shacks are charging only half as much."

"Well maybe she's worth it," Jake Harkins said, rubbing his chin thoughtfully.

"Maybe so," the complainer said. "But you just got into Dodge. Me and the boys have been here two weeks. The money's going fast."

"But she's really extra special," his companion said. "You'll see what I mean when she comes out. One of those dark-eyed beauties with a bosom you can see a mile away and those legs!"

"And wait till you see that underwear she's got on. Lace all over. A look at her underpants is enough to drive you wild."

At that moment the door of the shack opened and a tall cowboy wearing chaps and spurs came out smiling happily. As the door closed behind him he let out a great yawp of joy.

"How was she Martin?" one of the men asked.

"I just can't begin to tell you," the cowboy said. "She's just out of this world. You know till I met Frenchy I thought they were all like those ugly squaws and greasers they have in the other shacks. But this one's different."

"How different," one man pressed.

"Different in every department. First when she begins to peel. Well a lot of those dance hall girls—you know they pad their busts and everything. But when Frenchie begins to peel, you see right off that everything's she's got is absolutely real. What I mean is you not only see it with your eyes. You feel it. Then she smells so good. A lot of these honky-tonk girls are well just plain smelly. Never wash."

"Well how do you think you smell you old goat?" a man in the crowd said good-naturedly. "Especially after you been on a trail for two months. Why there've been nights on the trail when I had to move my bedroll away from you because the wind changed." "Sure I know," Martin said. "You ain't no rose yourself, Yancy. But a girl should be different. Hell, it ain't no fun sleeping with a smelly squaw, especially when the odor's so strong you can get wind of her half a mile away. Anyway, Frenchy's great. I can't recommend her highly enough, and if it's loving you want ..."

He was interrupted by the opening of the shack door. Instantly the roar of voices stopped. All eyes were glued to the doorway in which appeared a strikingly beautiful brunette.

It was not hard to understand the cowboy's superlatives. The girl had a face that combined a Gallic flavor with the coffee color and high cheekbones of the Caribbean natives. Her eyes were tiny pools of limpid beauty, dark and magnetic in their arrogance. Long black eye-lashes added to the exotic effect of the lovely face. Tiny, doll-like ears and a small childish mouth completed the startling effect. It was a face that was hard to forget and that was as different as night is from day from the blowsy, tired faces of the beer and whiskey swilling whores who plied their trade in the other shacks.

But this was not all, the men realized. Even in the darkness barely relieved by a dim oil lamp which cast its light from the interior, they could see her figure was superb. She wore only a bustle and long drawers of white linen with lace at the knees and the effect was electric. Her undergarments seemed barely to contain her hourglass figure and especially the magnificent round breasts and superb hips. The effect was crowned by a perfume which she had distributed liberally about her skin and garments and which the entranced cowboys inhaled like some heady incense.

For a long moment no one spoke. Then the girl herself broke the silence.

"You. Tall thin one. Come inside." She pointed a delicate finger at Johnny Blaise.

"Hey wait a minute," some one cried angrily. "I was here long before him. Let him wait his turn."

The girl looked at the new speaker and spat.

"There are plenty of other shacks. Frenchy takes whomever she wants."

Johnny reddened. "Listen lady. I appreciate your choice and all that but I'd just as soon let him visit with you first."

"No," the girl said firmly. "You or no one. Nobody tells me whom to take." She looked annoyed. "Make your mind up or I am leaving." She slammed the door behind her.

Johnny looked helplessly at the knot of impatient cowboys.

"Well hell it ain't none of my doing. You saw that. I'm not even anxious." He peered cautiously at their tense, silent faces.

Suddenly the tension was broken by the bull laugh of Jake Harkins.

"That's a good one. You ain't even too hungry and she's picking you." He slapped his thigh delightedly. "Well go on man. Don't keep the lady waiting. Go on."

"But Jake," the lanky cowboy protested. "All these boys were here before me. I can't just ..."

"Go on," several men cried. "She asked for you. Go in and keep her quiet. Last time she came to Dodge she left town like her tail was on fire."

Jake gave him a bottle and motioned to him to take a deep swig. Shrugging, Johnny did so. The harsh liquor inflamed him inside. Nodding toward the men, he opened the door of the shack and entered.

The interior of the shack surprised him. Usually there was little inside but a primitive bed and a chair. Aside from a carpet bag with the girl's belongings, the places looked empty. But Frenchy's place was different.

There was a small table covered with a beautiful green silk cloth and on it was a photograph of some city that Johnny did not recognize. A bottle of wine stood beside the picture.

On the walls of the shack were other pictures of cities— Johnny could not tell whether they were the same ones or not. The bed was covered by a coverlet of red cloth, a cloth that looked much finer than the usual calico you saw in such places. The air was perfumed so heavily, he felt as if he were in a room filled with flowers. It was a thick, heady perfume and it made him dizzy.

As soon as he entered, the girl smiled and opened a beautiful wooden box. He looked inside and saw little cigarettes. But these were tailor-made. And at the same time the box began to give out the notes of a lilting waltz. He stared at it amazed. Not so much at the cigarettes. The highly-polished box enchanted him. He picked it up and looked at it in sheer amazement.

"Where on earth is the music coming from?" he asked.

"There is a mechanism inside," she said smiling. "It's Swiss. One of my ami's in Mexico City brought it from Geneva for me. Have a cigarette, it will make you feel better."

"Thanks," he said helping himself. He broke off a match from the block in his pocket and lit their cigarettes. He inhaled deeply and shuddered. It was the strangest tobacco he had ever smoked. It tasted very odd and made him feel odd. He shook his head and smiled at the lovely girl who sat in her white drawers on the bed. Her superb figure was almost breathtaking and for a moment he stared at the gentle rising and falling of her substantial breasts.

"Come here Cherie," she said softly. "Come here and take me in your arms."

He rose unsteadily from his chair. The tobacco and the whiskey were making him really dizzy and he moved toward the girl at a rolling gait, almost as if he were a sailor on a storm-tossed ship. When he reached the bed he tripped over and fell into the girl's waiting embrace. She kissed him avidly, glueing her hot lips to his own and breathing into his mouth. The girl's arms were surprisingly muscular and strong and the feel of her body against his own made him tingle with excitement. He could feel the solid roundness of each breast pressing against his chest.

Blindly he began to grope for her, reaching instinctively for her flesh. As his fingers pierced the barrier of her bustle and he felt the warm skin of her bosom the girl groaned and pressed him harder to her torso.

"Aye Aye Aye!" she said. "You are a strong lover. I like you. I like you. You are not rough like those peasants outside who smell awful and treat a woman like she is an animal. Kiss me again."

He kissed her again and then instinctively began to pull her drawers away from her olive-skinned thighs. They fitted snugly.

She laughed childishly at his impatience. "Oh you cowboys, you are all so impatient. Wait, wait, you will rip it. It is my last pair from Paris. Let me do it. Smoke a little more. But inhale it deeply."

A moment later she was in his arms and the primitiveness of the shack, the knot of men waiting outside was completely forgotten as they reached for each other and lost themselves in a round of passionate kisses and embraces. He did not know what came over him. It was as if the world were spinning like a top and he was sitting on it. When it was over he lay back quietly and stared at the photographs on the wall.

"What town is that?" he asked calmly. "Mexico City?"

"No, Paris. My papa's birthplace. He was a soldier in Martinique where I was born. My mother was also an islander. Someday I hope to see it—Paris. My father used to talk about it always."

"Where is he now?" Johnny asked.

She did not speak for a moment. Then she said bitterly,

"He is dead. He died in Mexico where we had gone to live. The Mexicans shot him after Maximilian was executed. My mother and I were reduced to nothing. She had to live by taking in boarders and by teaching French to the sons of the Mexican officials. Hoping, hoping that one day she would make enough to take us both to Paris. To my father's people." The girl continued to talk as she lay on the coverlet beside him. The smoke from her cigarette curled lazily toward the ceiling as the light from the oil lamp worked magic on her bare skin. He had never seen anything so lovely as her oliveskinned body in that soft light. The girl's breasts glistened in the lamplight and her eyes shone like the eyes of a cat.

He coughed. "What is that tobacco. Something Mexican?"

"Yes. We call it marijuana. You like it?"

His eyes widened. "Is that marijuana? I've heard some of the Mexican vaqueros talk about it. But I've never had any myself. No wonder I feel funny."

"You do not find it pleasant?" she teased.

"Hell no," John said coughing. "I don't need that weed to get my head in the clouds. A few swigs of Texas Tanglefoot will do it."

He put out the cigarette and rose from the bed. "Thanks anyway beautiful. It was fun." He peeled a twenty dollar bill from the roll he carried and put it beside her.

"No, for you nothing" she said in a strange voice.

"But why?" he asked surprised. "I want to."

She shook her head. "I talked to you about my family. My father. I cannot accept money. Don't insist Cherie. It would hurt me very much. Just go and tell the others I must sleep for two hours. I am tired."

Johnny nodded sympathetically. "I guess you're right. But I sure hope these boys don't run off."

"No they will not," she said confidently. "Now kiss me once again and hold me as you did before."

He embraced her and kissed her. She held on to him with a tight grip and then, when he had let her go, brushed away a tear from her eyes.

"Go now cowboy. You remind me of a young American whom I loved once long ago in Mexico. He was a desperado and had come across the border. He had your eyes and your voice and your laugh and he made love like you. When you are with me in bed, I think it is him all over again."

He said nothing, understanding suddenly why she had chosen him for special consideration and why she would not take money now. He kissed her gently on the nose and said:

"Good luck to you Frenchy. Why don't you go to New Orleans? There must be many men who would give their eyes for a wife like you."

"Yes sometimes I think I will. But I am restless like you and cannot remain still long. This is why I like Dodge City I suppose."

"Goodby Frenchy," he said. "I'm glad, really glad you picked me. Will you be here long in Dodge?"

She shrugged, hesitated and then said: "For a while anyway. But not always here. I live a little away from the town when I am not here. If you need to, please come to me for anything. Take the road past the Johnson ranch. But come alone. Not with your cowboys."

He nodded. "Sleep well sweetheart." Outside Jake Harkins pumped his hand several times and laughed.

"I'm next," he cried excitedly. "How was it Johnny?"

"She's sleeping now Jake," he said. "Come back in a couple of hours."

"Hell's fires," Jake roared. "That's not fair. Well the hell with her, Johnny. Listen, I hear this Golden Burro is the best place in town. Let's go there, okay?"

Johnny shook his head. The fumes of the marijuana had made him unsteady. "I'd better lie down for a minute Jake. Don't get your dander up though. I'll be along. Save a good one for me."

Despite Jake's remonstrances, he insisted on meeting them later. After the big bullwhacker had left, he wandered down toward the river. The water glistened beautifully in the light of the full moon. Close to the Golden Burro he found a grassy knoll and lay down to nap. He felt extremely drowsy. Too drowsy to keep his eyes open long enough to get back to his hotel room.

He had no idea how long he slept. He could remember lying back and staring at the moon and the sounds of carousing that went on a short distance away. There were a few pistol shots. Then he must have fallen asleep. When he awoke he was startled to see a beautiful face peering down at him.

"Are you all right," the face said. He opened his eyes wider as he recognized Lola Flynn's pretty sister from Boston. He smiled.

"I'm fine now. I guess I dozed off a bit."

"I-l thought you were ill," she said. He was surprised at the musical quality of her voice. He stood up and dusted himself off.

"Well thanks for trying to help," he said smiling at her. Suddenly she recognized him and her face changed.

"It's you," she said annoyed. "The man at the hotel."

"Now look lady, I wasn't trying to do anything wrong. Listen if you're free I'd like some of your time. You're the prettiest thing I've ever seen in Dodge City. I never saw a girl wear clothes like that. You must have all the boys crazy."

He seized her in his arms and kissed her. She was so astonished that she did not resist until his lips were glued to hers. Then she pummeled him with her tiny fists and pushing away ran as fast as she could.

"Hey wait a minute honey," he yelled after her. "Maybe I should have waited till we got there."

He shook his head as he followed her fast retreating figure to the Golden Burro. He guessed she was angry because he had just grabbed her. When a dance hall girl is that pretty he thought, she wants special treatment. You don't just haul a girl like that up to the nearest room, or grab her in the street.

He sighed. Well he'd play it her way then. Hitching his pants, he moved resolutely toward the Golden Burro. He looked at the big frame building a quarter of a mile away and saw a group of cowboys saddle their horses to the hitch rail and saunter inside. One of them tried to stop Lola's sister as she approached the door. She slapped him so hard he fell into his neighbor's arms.

Johnny Blaise shook his head delightedly. This was a girl he had to know. He had never seen anyone so full of spirit.

CHAPTER THREE

You would not, even in your wildest mood, have classed the Golden Burro in Dodge City as a house of ill repute. Outwardly it resembled most gambling saloons. It had the same long bar, the nudes over the frosted mirror, rows of poker tables and a tiny stage that came alive at night with the high kicks of pretty dancing girls.

There was one difference, however, and it drew many patrons who might have gone elsewhere. The heavy players at poker and faro tables were served girls on the house.

There was cold logic behind this. Lola Flynn, the lovely red haired beauty who ran the place, reasoned that the presence of a beautiful and underclad girl at a player's shoulder helped him to continue gambling. Especially if the house insisted that the girl could not go to one of the upstairs bedrooms until 2 A.M.

On paper, at any rate, the system worked well. The player who sat at a table long enough knew that he could have his pick of the line of ladies available. The girls usually sat nearby and you could get anyone of them by nodding your head slightly. There was a good choice too. You could pick Frou Frou, the delicious Viennese dancer who had been stranded by a rich cattleman who fetched her from Europe, Dixie Knox, a singer from Chicago with a bosom that preceded her by a quarter of an hour, Sally Jones, the star of the biggest and most expensive bordello in New Orleans, a sultry mulatto with pear-shaped breasts from Havana, two farm girls from Iowa and a strapping wench with a 40-inch bust from Idaho. Sitting with them was the lovely, pinch-waisted saloon keeper, the doll-like Lola Flynn. Her long red tresses and pouting bosom drew more male eyes than all the rest. But, of course, she was not for sale.

The girl assigned to a player wore very little. The costumes could fit snugly into any purse. Dodge City, in those days, was not for the prudish. Half-dressed girls stood behind their men clutching excitedly the stray chips they were given as tips. There was no no fee for the girl's services, but the chips made a difference. If you took the girl upstairs at 2 A.M., she remembered those chips. There is nothing like gratefulness in lovemaking, as Lola always said. A well-tipped girl came through very loyally.

On paper then the system worked fine for everyone. The house kept its games going and the players could look forward to sleeping with any girl—except the gorgeous Lola of course—but the men had to keep playing till two. Too often, however, after several hours of knockdown and dragout poker and a dozen whiskies, a man's appetite was apt to evaporate along with his money.

By then many of the gamblers gave up the idea completely and tried to borrow enough money to pay their hotel bills. Lola was always very generous about this. She would offer up to ten dollars to anyone who needed to pay his hotel bill.

At the outset when Johnny Blaise entered the big central room of the Golden Burro he thought he was in some sort of theater.

There was a kind of stage at one end of the big hall and tables in front of it. On a mezzanine above there was a row of small boxes with red curtains, each box just big enough to hold two persons. That is two persons who sat fairly close to one another.

At the other end of the hall the gambling was centered. Peering through the thick knot of men standing at the far end, Johnny could see a wheel of fortune, faro, monte, chemin de fer and poker tables. Through the thick cigar smoke he noted that several games were in progress. He was looking around him uncertainly when a familiar voice greeted him. He turned and saw it was Buck Ranston.

"So you finally got here muchacho!" Buck said drunkenly. "We thought you'd never make it. What are you drinking? They got no Texas Tanglefoot in this place. Only something they call Forty-Yard."

"What the hell is Forty-Yard?" Johnny asked. He was glad to see a familiar face.

"Some new fermented juice. The bartender says reason they call it Forty-Yard is that it knocks you that far after two drinks. Want to try it cowboy?"

"Hell, sure. You're still on your feet ain't you?"

"That's because I've been sitting down and playing poker," Buck said. "You can't swallow Forty-Yard standing up."

"Come on Buck," Johnny heard a girl say plaintively. He saw Olive Gomez approach his friend from the other side. "They're waiting for you at the table."

"In a minute honey. In a minute. Gotta buy my old friend Johnny a drink. He looks cold sober and you know nobody can take this place cold sober."

He patted the Mexican girl affectionately on the rear and moved to the bar with his arm around Johnny's shoulders. Johnny saw Olive grimace but the Mexican did not stop him.

The bartender, an affable little fat man with sparse hair, greeted them with a welcoming grin and shook hands with Johnny.

"First drink for a new visitor to the Burro is on the house," he said. "Policy of the owner."

Johnny smiled his thanks, took the proffered drink and downed it quickly. He felt as if he had swallowed a Mexican hot pepper. The raw whiskey cauterized his insides as it entered his stomach and his face turned red.

Buck slapped his thigh and laughed. "What did I tell you boy? What did I tell you?"

"Have another Mr. Blaise?" the bartender said cautiously. He smiled and waited with the bottle in his hand.

Aware that Ranston was watching him carefully and that his failure to take two drinks would become a camp joke, he nodded. The second drink was equally volcanic in its effect. He had to resist his temptation to hold on to the bar.

Ranston shook his head in admiration. "That's doing it boy. I was telling Jake Harkins you probably couldn't make two."

"How many Jake have?" Johnny asked curiously.

"Three, but he had to lie down after that. Said he couldn't see his way back to the table. Nobody else has tried three at a time."

"How about you cowboy?" Olive Gomez said challengingly. "Let's see the boss man drink three if he's so strong."

"Shut up Olive," Buck said. "You want the man to fall down?"

"He's so strong he won't fall," Olive said sarcastically. "But I don't think he's that strong."

Johnny was aware that Olive's resentment stemmed from the beauty contest in the Triple Nugget saloon, but he was uncomfortably aware that several drinkers at the bar were listening.

"Don't pay any attention to her," Buck said. "Don't do it boy. That stuff's like gun powder. Try one in about half an hour."

"That's right cowboy," Johnny heard a brassy male voice bellow at the other end of the bar. "Play it safe. You don't want to get hit with a poleaxe. Your friends might have to carry you out like that bullwhacker."

Johnny reddened and turned toward the source of the sarcasm. He saw the tenderfoot he had collided with in Greene's hotel earlier. The big man's face was full of contempt as he stood there. Johnny had a wild impulse to move over to the nattily dressed Easterner and knock him down. But at the same moment he saw Lola Flynn's sister approach with another girl and hesitated.

"Let's go Johnny," Buck said hurriedly. He was afraid of what the third drink might do to his friend and he was afraid that Johnny's impulsiveness might drive him to heedlessness.

Johnny pursed his lips and stared thoughtfully at the well-cut frock coat and golden chain of the other man. He sensed the quickened interest of the two women beside him.

"I'll tell you what stranger," Johnny said at last. "A hundred dollars says I stand up longer than you. You willing to drink on that?"

"Don't do it Sam," he heard Lola's sister say. "He wants to get you drunk so he can force you to draw against him."

Billings laughed and patted the girl's arm affectionately. Then he turned to Lola. "Lola, did you tell your sister that I was the best shot in my regiment?" He smiled at the younger girl. "Don't worry Penny. If he tries to draw it'll be the last move he ever makes."

Turning to Johnny he said. "Let's see the color of your money, Texas." He took a roll of bills from his coat pocket and handed them to the bartender. "Hold that."

Johnny gave the bartender a like amount and smiled politely at Penny Flynn.

"Don't fret lady. I don't shoot drunks. And if I did I wouldn't do it here." He nodded reassuringly to Buck who nodded back as if to say he was ready if there was trouble. The contest had attracted a number of by-standers, and a moment later Jake Harkins hove into view.

"Johnny don't do it," he said. "I got a stronger stomach than you and this man's bigger than both of us. If you want to bet a hundred do it on a fight maybe. You might take him that way even if he has the reach on you. But that whiskey'll knock you flat. Besides he's been here drinking the stuff before probably."

"I'm sure Mr. Billings will forget the whole matter if you wish," Lola said smiling. "Give them back their money Jenkins."

"Yes," Penny said, smiling at Johnny's discomfiture. "That Forty-Yard's a man's drink. I don't want him to turn green. I may have to get my smelling salts."

The remark triggered a round of laughter on all sides. Johnny reddened and nodded firmly toward the bartender. "Let's go Jenkins. I'll start first."

The bartender shrugged and served him a drink. Jake Harkins and Buck Ranston waited expectantly. They had known it was useless to try to dissuade Johnny. He was the most impulsive man they knew and would rather risk his life than pass up a challenge. Any kind of challenge. But particularly one where women watched the outcome of the contest.

The third drink made Johnny so rocky he had to hold on to the bar. He saw Billings down his own with relative ease. The next one made him so dizzy the room and its occupants swam in a kind of kaleidoscope. Billings' sardonic face was the only thing that kept him going. He was pleased however to notice that the Easterner's voice sounded fuzzy when he asked him if he wished to continue.

The next drink cut him off from his moorings almost completely. He wanted to sit down on the floor. Only a stubborn streak inside him kept him up. If he had been ready to yield to temptation, Penny's voice stopped him. He heard her say:

"You'd better hold him. He's going to fall down."

"Gimme another one," he rasped to the waiting bartender. He swallowed it and despite the thundering in his temples remained upright. How he did he did not know. He had been on numerous drinking bees with cowboys, but he had not drunk anything as potent as this stuff.

"One more Mr. Billings," the bartender said quietly.

The Easterner looked glassily at the man behind the counter and nodded. He downed it and shuddered. His head inclined toward the table.

The bartender put another drink in Johnny's hand and summoning up some willpower he did not know he possessed he swallowed it. He was unable to see anything, but the words of Penny Flynn continued to goad him.

"One for you Mr. Billings?" Jenkins asked. The big man in the frock coat, his hair mussed, his eyes unseeing, gave an affirmative answer. The crowd, swelled to a much larger number watched him tensely. Billings moved the drink unsteadily toward his mouth his hand shaking so much he spilled several drops. Finally he was able to pour the contents of the glass between his lips.

He smiled to the crowd and then without warning sank to the ground. The watchers stared at him and then turned to look at Johnny.

"You did it you son-of-a-gun," Jake Harkins exulted. "You did it! How do you feel?"

"Wonderful Jake," Johnny said, a foolish grin on his face. Slowly he turned to the bartender, and held out his hand. Jenkins reached out to give him the money but before he could transfer the greenbacks, the Texan slumped to the floor and lay beside Billings. A moment later he was snoring peacefully. Buck Ranston took the winnings and stuffed them into the buckskin sack tied to his belt. Then he and Jake Harkins carried the lanky cowboy toward the exit.

"No need to do that," Lola said. "Take him to one of the rooms upstairs. He can sleep it off. Ask the cook for a pot of coffee if you like.

"Thank you ma'am," Jake said. As they lugged the sleeping youth up the stairs he shook his head. "Son you're going to have to tone down a little. You ain't made of iron."

"You ain't a wolfing," Buck said. "He's been moving around Dodge like a horse on loco weed ever since we got here. Between the juice he's swallowed and the girls he's taken in tow, he hasn't had a moment's rest in 48 hours. I'll be damned if I know how he keeps going."

"Well don't sell the Blaise's short. You ever go anywhere with his brother Tom? He can drink anybody under the table and play poker around the clock. I wished he'd come up with us. But he don't like Dodge much. Says they're out to skin you alive and too many Yankees for his taste."

"Too bad. Tom'd like the Golden Burro," Buck said. "He likes the cards and he wouldn't go wrong with the women neither. Say who you going upstairs with?"

"Hell I haven't given it much thought. There's a big girl stands behind my table all the time. I'd like to try her. But you can't take them up for another five hours yet. I don't know if I can last that long. Maybe I'll go back to the "line" and try Frenchie. She'll be back after a while."

Buck shook his head as they lay the sleeping boy on a bed. "I don't think we ought to leave Johnny alone like this. Besides I'm losing. I gotta stick around or I'll go back home with nothing but my britches, Jake.

"Who you aiming to sleep with Buck, that little Mexican? I'll bet she's something with those clothes off, and passionate too."

"She's fine" Buck said smiling. "But the one I'd like to climb in the haystack with is the big madam here. Little old Lola. You noticed how she looks when she bends over the poker tables. Mister Harkins, I really thought both those things would just pop out right there. And I caught a look at her legs when she bent over. Most beautiful legs you ever saw. I'd give a lot to see Lola without her duds on."

"Well, don't hold your breath son. I don't think Lola gives it away. You'll have to take one of the other girls."

"Well, her little sister ain't so bad either."

"I think Billings is bedding with her. You notice how he looks daggers at any man who even glances at her too long?"

Jake sighed. "Just give me Frenchy for a couple of hours. Just smelling her bare skin makes me drunk, son. I heard one of the boys waiting outside say that she dunks herself naked as a jaybird in the river up a ways from town. With some servant girl holding guard over her with a Winchester. That must be a lovely sight, seeing Frenchy's wet body coming up out that water. Ain't much chance though I guess."

"Why don't you offer to scrub her back Jake," Buck suggested. "Tell her you'll bring the soap and keep your mind strictly on your work."

The two men left their friend to sleep it off and returned three hours later with a pot of coffee. They woke him and gave him some of the strong, hot brew and some sandwiches put together hastily in the kitchen. Johnny smiled at them despite his hangover and devoured the sandwiches greedily.

"How you feeling son," Jake asked in a kindly voice? "You up to poker? They got a lot of our money downstairs. Maybe you can win some of it back."

Johnny yawned. "Sure. Love to play." He closed his eyes.

"Let him sleep a little longer, "Buck whispered. "There's plenty of time."

Jake nodded and moved toward the door.

About an hour later, Johnny was awakened by the sound of women quarreling in the adjoining room. He rose from the bed chuckling. They were probably two of the girls who went upstairs with the gamblers. He might as well see what they looked like and whether they compared favorably with Frenchy or Lola's sister. If they did not then the Golden Burro had no more to offer than any other dance hall. He and Jake and Buck might as well move somewhere else.

He kneeled by the keyhole and peered through it. What he saw made him suck in his breath. Lying on the bed in her long white drawers was Penny Flynn. She was lying on her back, her arms folded behind her head. John was amazed at how beautiful her breasts were. They looked like the softest, creamiest mounds he had ever seen. Then he realized they could not have been too soft. As she lay there her whole body radiated a firmness that told him there was not an inch of flabby flesh in her young, healthy body. Her breasts were sheer miracles. They looked as if they had been designed by some sculpture genius, by a a great artist who wanted to create perfection in the female form. But this was no statue. This was a young, beautiful and very much alive young woman. And moreover a young woman who was extremely cross.

"I don't know why I can't wear those French bosom cups," she was saying petulantly to someone he could not see. "No one will see them. But they feel so wonderful. The softest, sheerest silk I've ever felt. Please let me wear them."

"I can't darling," another female voice said. "I only have two pair. A Frenchman on his way to California gave them to me. One of them needs some sewing and I'm wearing the other. Besides darling you're much too big there. These are made for smaller bosoms."

"Yes," Penny said unhappily. "I guess I am too big there. Do you think they look ugly?"

"No of course not. How silly," Lola laughed.

"You don't think my husband ... I mean the man I marry will find me too big there?" Penny persisted.

"Oh you child. Men love that. You know something I envy you. I wish I had your bosom."

"You're not ugly there Lola. And I haven't noticed any men look the other way when you wear your deep neck gowns."

"You silly goose," Lola said. "What on earth makes you talk about bosoms so much?"

"Oh I dont' know," the younger girl said. She began to giggle and Johnny nearly fell to the floor as he watched her mounds rise and fall. "I guess it's because so many of the girls have complimented me on my figure."

"What else have they told you?" Lola said sharply. She came closer to the bed and Johnny blinked. She was wearing bust guards or something, that was almost completely transparent. He could see at once that Lola Flynn had no reason to fear competition from her sister. Her breasts seemed as big as melons even through the keyhole. But that was not all that astonished him.

Instead of the long opaque white drawers Penny wore, Lola wore pantaloons of a pink silk that clung possessively to her plump hips and milk-white thighs. The sight of her seductively curved hips and halfmoons of her rear made him feel warm.

There was no doubt about it, the Golden Burro's girls were something. The stories he had heard were all true. And he was pleased that his hunch about Penny Flynn's shape without her clothes was right. She was superb. He dismissed a flicker of guilt about watching them through the keyhole. After all why not? They were both prostitutes weren't they? And this was just another version of the kind of parlor house that abounded in Dodge. The trouble was that usually you got no chance to see if a dance hall girl was not faking her charms till you had hired her to go upstairs. It wasn't often you got a buyer's look like this.

"Get dressed Penny and go home with Frank," Lola said. "I've got to get dressed myself." She bent over to do something to her shoes and Johnny saw her lift up her perfectly shaped legs to put her stockings on. The sight of those legs would make any man unsteady he thought. All the same he preferred Penny who had stood up now and was carefully examining her upright breasts in the mirror.

She began to dress slowly, reluctantly. Johnny Blaise took his eyes away from the door. He had just realized that Penny Flynn had a completely false notion of what went on in the Golden Burro or in any other dance hall in Dodge. He was surprised, but her sister's next words helped him to understand better.

"You were a fool to come out here from Boston. This is no place for you Penny."

"I'm not sorry I came. These last few weeks have been the most exciting ones in my life. They'll never believe me in Boston. If I ever go back to Boston that is."

"Of course you'll go back," Lola stormed. "I told you you could stay till Independence Day. Then you're being put on that

Santa Fe train whether you like it or not. Unless of course you change your mind about Sam Billings."

"I won't change my mind," Penny said flatly. "He doesn't interest me as a husband," Penny's voice mounted to shrill anger.

"You're a fool" he sister retorted. "You'd be lucky to find a man in Boston half the man he is. And he's going to be rich. Do you know how much land the syndicate he heads owns? And what the railroads will pay for it?"

"Why don't you marry him yourself Lola?"

"He's not interested in me," Lola said. "Anyway I'm not interested in marriage. I'm happy as I am."

"Running a dance hall you mean?" Penny said scornfully. "Why don't you come back to Boston with me Lola?"

"I can't stand Boston and I hate Yankees."

"Then at least go back to Savannah where you know everyone," Penny pleaded. "What is the sense of staying out here where there's nothing but drunken cowboys and gamblers. What kind of life is this for you?"

"I could never go back to Savannah," Lola said in a choked voice. "You think I could live there after what the Yankees did."

"I'm sorry," Penny said contritely. "I didn't mean to remind you. I just wanted to get you away from here."

They were interrupted by a knock on the door.

"Yes?" Lola asked impatiently.

"It's Dabney," a male voice said. "I've got to see you."

"Just a moment," Lola said. "Go on home Penny. Frank's waiting downstairs. And if any of those drunken cowboys bother you let me know."

Johnny heard Penny say goodnight and then close the door behind her. He heard a man greet her, but could not recognize the voice.

"That's a pretty sister you have," the visitor said lightly.

"You didn't come here to talk about my sister," Lola said annoyed. "Get to the point Dabney."

Johnny moved away from the door and began to smooth his shirt and hair. He wasn't interest in listening to Lola and her lover. He wondered if there were some way he could see Penny now.

A moment later as he got ready to leave, he heard the man with Lola say, "I'm sorry, Lola. I had to see you."

"It better be important," Lola expostulated. "I told you not to come here. You might as well tell the Marshall what we're up to when he comes."

"That's just it," the newcomer said. "He's not coming next week. He's coming tomorrow."

"Tomorrow?" Lola said astonished. "But we got the word from Kansas City that he wasn't due till Wednesday. Are you sure?"

"Absolutely. My source knows every move he makes. He's with him all the time."

"What's his program?" Lola said suddenly.

Johnny shrugged and moved to the door. Suddenly he stopped as he heard the next words of the visitor.

"First Sherman will visit the cattle camps outside of town. Then he'll tour the Arkansas River valley up to about twenty miles from Dodge. But there's been one thing added. He'll be here long enough to spend the night. He doesn't get off till eight A.M. the next morning."

"Fat chance of doing anything with the Masterson brothers both in town as well as a detachment of soldiers from the fort," Lola said drily.

"Don't you worry," Dabney said. "The Yankee bastard won't get out of Dodge alive. I can guarantee that. It's all arranged. Come here, I'll show you."

Johnny Blaise glued his eye to the keyhole again. He could see Lola standing in the middle of the room and next to her a tall man.

He couldn't make the man's features out.

"Please don't tell me or show me anything," Lola said irritably. "Do what you must do, but don't involve me in any way."

"It's too late to talk that way honey. You were interested when I told you about it three weeks ago when we first heard Sherman was coming."

"I was angry," Lola said annoyed. "I never thought anything would come of it. Take the money and go for heaven's sake. I don't want anyone to know you were here."

A moment later Johnny heard the man sigh. "Thanks Lola. This will be enough to pay our man. Let me tell you what we're going to do."

"No," Lola pleaded. "Leave me out of it."

The man laughed. "Okay, never mind. Come here and give us a kiss."

"Please. Not now. Anyone might come in. There are people downstairs."

"The hell with them. Come here."

Johnny listened to the sounds of lovemaking next door and cursed. If only she had kept her mouth shut. He was going to tell her everything.

Suddenly he heard Jake Harkins' voice in the corridor.

"Johnny? You awake yet? It's Jake. Come on boy. Time's awasting."

"Get going for heaven's sake," he heard Lola say in a frightened voice.

"You going to keep your mouth shut about this, Lola so long as you're not in with us?" the man said coldly.

"Of course."

"You'd better or we'll keep it shut permanently."

"Johnny!" Jake began to holler. "Come on boy!"

Johnny groaned inwardly.

"You gonna sleep all night?" Jake said through the door.

CHAPTER FOUR

"Hey Johnny?" Jake yelled again in a blurred voice. "You awake or not? You're passing up all the fun. We got girls down there comin' out of both ears, boy."

Johnny remained absolutely still by the keyhole.

"You'd better get going," Lola said frightened. "I don't want them to see you? Don't use that door or he'll see you. Use the other one."

"Why?" the man said carelessly. "Who cares what a drunken Texas idiot thinks. You're entertaining a man in your room. So what?"

"I'm entertaining one of Quantrill's old raiders," Lola said. "So what. We did it for the South. Including Texas."

"Never mind that. If the colonel at Fort Dodge knew I was entertaining any of Quantrill's old gang, he'd have me shut up in twenty-four hours."

"Stop worrying. Nobody knows my real name," the man said.

Johnny heard no more. At that moment the door of his room burst inward and Jake Harkins came in. He struck his knee against a chair in the darkness and cursed loudly.

"Where the hell are you Johnny?" Jake roared. "I almost lost a leg. Put the lamp on will you?"

Johnny lit the oil lamp with a shake of his head. That damned fool Jake. If he had only held his water a few seconds longer he might have known what they planned to do with General Sherman and when.

He yawned audibly as he lit the lamp and then stretched out on the bed. "What the hell are you bellowing like a bull for Jake?" he said very loudly in a tone of sharp annoyance. He raised his voice as he continued: "Holy Peter can't a man sleep? What the hell are you pounding on the door like that for. You scared me out of a year's growth. I was in the middle of a wonderful dream."

"Probably a wet one if I know you," Jake said laughing. "Come on down and play cards son. Me and Buck's practically giving it away. Anyway Buck asked me if you could give us a stake for a few more hands. That is if you got any left yourself."

"Sure," Johnny said readily. He took some money from his leather sack and handed it to his friend. "But if I was you I wouldn't play much longer. You can hardly stand up, and you almost missed me with the light on. Go on and tell how in the name of heaven you can see those cards. I'll bet you can't even read your own hand."

Harkins looked hurt. "Sure I can. I may be drunk but I'm not blind. I've been eating some beef along with that raw alcohol they serve here. You coming down to play Johnny?"

"No, I think I'll mosey on up to the hotel," Johnny said. "I promised to write Tom a letter about the herd and give it to one of the boys heading back in the morning."

Jake scratched his wooly head. "I wish you'd play a few hands Johnny. I hate to see those bastards haul off and take all our money. You always did have good luck at poker. Besides Lola asked about you a while back. She'll think it strange if you just walk out like that. Like you don't like her place or nothin'."

Johnny stiffened. Of course, Jake was right. Lola would think his absence strange and might even make her wonder if he had been eavesdropping in the next room. Maybe he'd better show his face at the tables and take an interest in gambling. He controlled an impulse to rush back toward Greene's hotel and try to intercept Lola's sister. Maybe she could identify the visitor in Lola's room. Unless he knew who the man was and what he would be doing tomorrow, it might be hard to stop anything from happening.

"Let's go down Jake," he said tightening his belt. "I guess I ought to play a few hands."

"Damn right you ought.

The gambling area was noisy and alive when they reached it. Above the hub-bub of bull whackers, mule skinners, cowboys and freighters, Johnny could hear the brassy voices of the dealers yelling out the cards in Monte and poker.

The moment he appeared Buck Ranston pulled a chair for him at one of the green poker tables and introduced him to the other players. There was Big Stick Harry Spaulding, called that because he carried a walnut cane; Tom Bilding, a railroad agent, Skipper O Toole who had piloted a Confederate freighter in the Gulf of Mexico during the war and Colonel Sam Hooser, a former Southern cavalry officer from Tennessee. The dealer was a swarthy looking man whom everybody called Frisco because he had come from San Francisco the year before.

As the hands were dealt, various girls came up to help individual players. Either by watching their hands or serving them drinks. None of them talked much however. Playing poker was serious business in Dodge and no one in his right mind thought otherwise. But it was all right to feel the girlies' waists once in a while or admire their busts and to wink occasionally as a reminder that when the game was over they could play together upstairs.

The men were so engrossed in the game that they barely looked up when Lola did her second show of the evening. It was watched mostly by the hangers-on at the long bar and a group of visitors sitting at tables in the other end of the room. Johnny taught a glimpse of two or three tables filled with soldiers in uniform who were having a gay time at the far end of the big hall. One of the soldiers was doing a drunken jig while several of his comrades clapped hands enthusiastically.

On the stage six of the girls, dressed in brief costumes that showed most of their shapely legs were doing a high kick to the music from the piano player. The men at the card tables glanced at the kickers with mild amusement and then turned back to their hands. It was useless. Lola had a way of forcing men to look at her. Especially when she danced.

The beautiful red head, wearing an elegant crinoline gown of crimson with spangles on it sang several love songs accompanying the words to a lilting dance step. Every so often she would whirl about the stage in a maneuver that would send her voluminous skirts billowing and reveal her beautifully curved legs. Her decolletage was cut so deep that when she took her bows, you could see the round firmness of her breast.

While she was on the games lagged. Not even the grimfaced Frisco prodded the players to tell him their bets or how many cards they wanted.

Skip O'Toole, a giant of a man with a heavy blond beard and hair to match, expressed the sentiment of all when he said wistfully: "What I wouldn't give to take Lola upstairs and take them duds off. What I wouldn't give. Making love to that girl would be like going to heaven on a flying horse, no fooling."

"Simmer down Skip," Colonel Sam said, biting hard on a long brown cigar. "All of us would like to get between the sheets with Lola. She just isn't for sale that's all."

"How about that cute-faced sister of hers," Big Stick Harry asked curiously, tilting his long face at the dealer. "Any chance of getting her upstairs. I sure wouldn't mind trying her for size. Mighty pretty."

Johnny Blaise found himself getting angry to his surprise. What the hell did it matter to him what Penny Flynn did. She was just another girl who was built for a man's hands to measure and play with. Who the devil cared what anyone wanted to do with her. All the same he discovered he was getting hot under the collar when Frisco said in his brassy voice.

"Listen Harry. I've got the hots for Penny too. I caught a look at her legs yesterday when she was bending over the table. The girl's built like a champion. Curves all over and a temper like a Mexican hot pepper. But Lola looks fit to kill if any man jack even looks at her too long. About the only man excepted is Sam Billings. I think Lola hopes Penny'll marry him."

"You think he's getting much?" Big Stick Harry asked.

"Well he's a crazy fool if he's got a clear track and don't get his hands on that," Jake said laughing. "That girl would make me forget to eat."

"Let's play cards for Pete's sake," Johnny said irritably. The others looked at him curiously but said nothing.

He played several hands without winning and then his luck began to change. Then, just as the cards began to come his way, he saw Big Stick Harry push back his chair, slap the substantial backside of a tall, robust blonde and motion toward the stairs. The blonde nodded, giggling. Skip O'Toole picked a pretty Mexican girl a moment later and was followed by Sam Hooser who selected a big, broad-hipped farmgirl.

"Where you all going?" Johnny asked amused.

"Grab yourself a girl Johnny and come upstairs with us," Buck said, putting his arm around Olive Gomez. "You can take one of the rooms or one of the boxes according to your pleasure."

"You mean the games are finished?" Johnny said surprised.

"No, no," Frisco said. "Just go on as usual. Lola's rule is that steady players can take any of the girls upstairs for a while after two A.M. that's all. They'll be back. So will I." He rose, put on his coat and lit a cigar. "Be back in half an hour."

"Well where are the dealers if I want to keep playing," Johnny complained. "The place sounds dead. Like it's ready to close up."

"Take a look around son," Frisco said cooly.

To his surprise, Johnny saw several beautiful dance hall girls take the dealers' chairs at different tables. Although the tables remained only half or two-thirds empty, the games kept going.

Soon there was the familiar sounds of gambling around him: the shuffling of silver dollars, the slap of decks, the click of checks tossed into the pot and the whirring roll of the big wheel of fortune.

Lola had decided wisely that the gambling operation had to be relaxed after two A.M. The men who wanted to go to bed with a girl between hands were obliged. The male dealers who had been working for hours were given time for a snack and a quiet smoke. And to keep the players who preferred playing happy, she let the girls who weren't undressing upstairs take over the dealers' slots.

The girls wore very low-cut gowns and their breasts were barely hidden by peekaboo handkerchiefs which managed to show everything a girl had whenever she moved. At Johnny's table the girl's bosom was so big, it looked ready to burst out of her gown whenever she moved.

Three of the seats that were vacant were taken by newcomers who had wandered in from Long Branch or Kelly's saloons nearby.

They had obviously been drinking and were unsteady on their feet.

They called for new cards in blurred, almost indecipherable voices and lost money pot after pot without seeming even to notice it.

As the game progressed, new players joined in. One was a grizzled old prospector who wore a buckskin shirt and introduced himself as Mike Saunders, lately from Leadville, Colorado. He was completely sober and watched the dealer with shrewd eyes. Johnny watched him amusedly.

"How's it going cowboy?" a familiar voice said at his shoulder. He looked up to find Lola Flynn smiling down at him.

"Just great Lola," he grinned in return. "You have a nice place here." He was glad she had noticed him. Now he could take off.

"Thanks. How come you didn't take one of the girls upstairs. I got a pretty Mulatto from New Orleans free if you're in the mood."

"No," Johnny said. "I guess I'm a little too tired. Besides I hate to bust into a winning streak." As soon as she left, he would finish the hand and head for the hotel, he thought. He had to see Penny.

Lola smiled. "I understand. Well if you change your mind let me know. Her name is Rose. She's a big girl and ..."

Lola stopped suddenly and looked down at the floor. One of the new players was on his hands and knees. She kicked him playfully on the behind. "What do you think you're doing Bill?"

Bill got up laughing and looked bleary-eyed at her. "Well, Lola, it's like this. I bet a man at the Triple Nugget yesterday that your girl dealers wore French pants instead of them long white drawers the town women wear. But I didn't get a chance to see if I won or not."

"Stand up Lottie," Lola ordered, "and show Bill whether he won his bet or not."

The amazon at the poker table rose cooly and lifted her skirts until they were above her waist. Everyone could see she was wearing green underdrawers of some flimsy, almost transparent cloth. They were short and left most of her beefy, milk-white thighs free. Bill nodded happily.

"Satisfied?" Lola asked casually. "Lottie generally charges five dollars for a look like that Bill."

"Thanks Lola. I just won ten dollars. But I can win fifty if I see something else?"

"What's that?" Lola asked curiously.

Bill laughed sheepishly. "I bet fifty dollars you got a strawberry birthmark on your backside."

The remark triggered a round of heavy laughter around the table. Even Mike Saunders lost some of his serious mein, and smiled. Johnny nearly fell out of his chair when he saw the surprise on Lola's face.

"Well that's one bet you'll have to forget about," she said crisply.

"You mean there ain't any such mark?" Bill asked.

"I'm not telling or showing," Lola retorted. "Now get back to your cards."

"Aw come on Lola be a sport," someone at an adjoining table said. "I'm willing to double that bet. I say you don't have one. I never saw a fair-skinned girl have a mark there."

"I'll take that bet," another voice yelled.

"How about you sir?" Mike Saunders said to Johnny. "Would you like to bet on Lola's—er—anatomy?"

"Sure why not?" Johnny said good-naturedly. "Fifty says she has got a mark on her bottom."

In a moment at least a dozen other bets were made. The last, by a tall, handsome man who stood a few feet away from the table. Johnny turned as he heard the familiar voice. It was Bat Masterson.

"Come on Lola. There's too much money riding on your bottom now. You better show your fanny or there won't be any games here the rest of the evening."

"That's right," several voices cried. "No bottom, no poker."

"Go on Lola," Johnny said wickedly. "I'm sure you've got nothing to hide. Besides there's no sense in being shy. After all your girls are doing it upstairs."

There was another roar of drunken laughter. Lola glared angrily at Bat Masterson and Johnny Blaise. Then without a word she turned her back to them. A hush fell over the big room as she raised her voluminous skirts slowly. When they were high enough to reveal her pink underdrawers, several whistles were heard and a number of men raised their bets. She barely gave them time to examine her strong, white thighs and the shapely half-moons of her buttocks. It was enough though to make several players sober.

A few seconds later Lola rolled down the top of her flimsy, flesh-clinging panties. There for everyone to see was a strawberry-colored birthmark. Instantly Lola adjusted her underthings and her skirts. Then throwing them all a contemptuous look, she marched off angrily. At the foot of the stairs she gave Johnny a look of the utmost loathing and then climbed upwards quickly, as a round of hearty applause began. Bat sat down laughing.

Bat Masterson shook his head. "I guess Lola doesn't love either of us tonight Johnny. But hell there wasn't any call for her to act so coy. Everyone knows this is a honky-tonk where you can have any of her girls in the rooms or in the boxes upstairs. What's she acting like the Governor's wife for?"

Johnny took the new hand dealt him and said suddenly: "Bat I've got to speak to you right away. Alone. Something urgent."

"Sure," Bat said, taking his own hand. "Let's just finish the hand and then we can have a drink over there."

The hand was a poor one for Johnny and when Mike raised the ante he threw it in. Pretty soon it was a race between Bat and Mike. Johnny watched Mike take three cards and carefully study them.

"Let me have one of the sandwiches on that plate Lottie," Mike said suddenly. "I'm hungry."

Lottie reached boredly behind her and took a sandwich which she gave to Mike. A moment later, as he bit into it, he laid his cards down. He had three aces and two kings against Bat's three Jacks. He began to shovel in the pile of silver dollars on the table.

"Wait a minute," Bat said in a hard voice. "Give me that sandwich."

"I'm eating it," Mike protested. "Get one of your own."

Bat grabbed it from his hands. In between the slices of bread were two half eaten cards.

"Get up Mike," he ordered, drawing his gun. "I thought it was you. That mustache doesn't change your face much. It's still as ugly as ever."

Mike Saunders got up sheepishly. Bat Masterson stiffened as he saw the other players reach for their guns.

"Don't get excited boys. This is government business." He pulled Mike's gun.

The men relaxed. "Empty your pockets Mike. Fast."

When the cheater had piled his winnings on the table, Bat divided it into neat piles, one for each man at the table. Then he motioned to Mike to move toward the door ahead of him. "Want to give me a hand, Johnny?" Bat asked casually. Johnny rose quickly and followed.

"That's the first time I've seen Bat Masterson call for help in bringing a man in," the female dealer said softly. "Next time you'll probably have to have Wyatt Earp with you. Too bad he's gone."

Bat smiled, twirled his cane in farewell and left, pushing Mike ahead of him. Outside Bat said tersely:

"Mike I ought to shoot. You know that?"

"Yep," he said sadly.

"I will next time I see you." He gave Mike five dollars in silver and said. "You better ride hell for leather in any direction Mike. If any of these boys see you in daylight, you'll look like a sieve. Now get!"

"Thanks Bat," Mike said with the air of a deacon. He walked to his horse, a few yards away and disappeared into the darkness of the empty prairies.

Bat shook his head. "Poor Mike, I feel sorry for him. His trick is getting to be so well known in the West that he can't make any money. I saw him pull the same trick—eating the cards in Abilene about six months ago. They call him 'Eat Em Up Mike' there. He's a cheat, but he usually plays for small stakes, so I can't hate him too much. Now what's on your mind Johnny?"

Taking a deep breath in the night air, Johnny told him the conversation he had heard upstairs at the Golden Burro.

Bat Masterson listened thoughtfully as he played with his cane. When it was over he nodded.

"I've been worried about that myself. But till now I didn't even have a lead on what they might be planning. When the commandant at Fort Dodge told me Sherman was coming this way I nearly jumped out of my shirt. Dodge City has about ten former Rebs to one Yankee and lots of them lost kin in the war."

"No," Bat said thoughtfully. "I don't think it would help Dodge City much either. If a man as big as General Sherman were murdered here, they'd slap martial law on us so fast it would make your head swim. The Governor has threatened to call Federal troops in a few times to halt the shootings. And if they did that the town might as well fold up. The Texans love this town because it's wide open. You can play cards, get drunk or make love around the clock and nobody stops you unless you get nasty. Hell that's why I like it."

He paused. "I've been wondering what action to take while I talked. Let's see, Sherman's in Wichita now."

CHAPTER FIVE

He poked his stick at the ground as he thought.

"We have to have time to learn their moves and find out who the killer or killers are," he said at last. "The commandant at Fort Dodge told me Sherman will arrive at Fort Larned early tomorrow morning. That is in about six or eight hours. He's traveling with a group of Army officers. We've got to keep him at Larned a day or two. I can't go and frankly I wouldn't know whom to send. Whoever is behind this, Lola or someone else is probably watching my moves. I can't let anything happen to Sherman. I'd have to quit as marshall. I've got to stop them."

"Let me go," Johnny said. "I can make it in about four hours of hard riding." He was anxious to help Masterson, more than ever since he was a friend of his brother's.

"No," Masterson said. "They know you too well now. You were upstairs. They might guess you heard and were going to warn Sherman. How about one of your friends? Someone you can trust."

Johnny thought for a moment. "Most of the boys are either drinking around town or sleeping it off somewhere. I'd have to locate them. But Jake Harkins and Buck Ranston are in the Burro."

"Let's get them. Or rather you get them and bring them over to my office. I'll have a note for the commander at Fort Larned ready. But we'll have to move fast. There isn't time to lose."

Johnny shook hands and headed quickly for the Golden Burro. The bartender was surprised to see him come back.

"Ready for some more poker friend?" he asked.

"No thanks. I came to find my companeros. You see them?"

The man motioned toward the ceiling. "They're all up there, amigo," he said. "But I wouldn't disturb them now if I was you. There are times when a man does not like to be disturbed."

Johnny did not bother to answer. He took the stairs two at a time and began to call for Jake and Buck. There was no reply. He knocked brusquely at one of the doors in the corridor and received a bellow from Skip O'Toole.

"What the hell do you want? I'm busy."

"You know where Jack Harkins and Buck Ranston are?" Johnny asked.

"Down the hall. Last two rooms, I think."

He wandered down the corridor and knocked. There was no answer. He knocked again and finally in desperation pushed in the door. Buck Ranston was sleeping peacefully on the bed. Standing beside him, wearing only an angry look, was Olive Gomez.

"You cowboys!" she spat venomously. "You are all alike. You drink, drink, drink, and then are good for nothing."

She was furious with Buck for caving in as soon as they reached the upstairs room. She stood there naked and beautiful. Her coffee-colored breasts and legs boldly demanding his attention, her hands on her bare hips.

"Look at me!" she ordered. "Do I look like a woman a man falls asleep on like that? As if I were a cow? Madre mia! I could kill him for that."

Johnny nodded sympathetically and turned away. He had to find Jake. But Olive was not ready to let him go. Moving up to him, she threw her arms around him.

When he came to the morning sun was streaming through the windows and he could hear the heavy breathing of Jake Markins on the bed.

Johnny. I will be good for you. I promise. Please stay and give me some money."

He disengaged her hands politely. At another time her young, athletic body with its perfectly shaped globes and haunches would have made it difficult for him to leave. But this was an emergency. He could not stay another moment.

"No, Johnny," the Mexican girl pleaded. "Don't go. Please don't go. I want you to stay." She had counted on the extra money Buck would give her as a gift.

"Some other time honey," he said. "I got to find Jake now."

Going back to the hall, he tried the other door. Again there was no answer. He forced his way in again. He saw Jake Harkins stretched out on the bed in his underclothes. He was alone in the room. Going up to him he lifted Jake's head. The man groaned softly as he opened his eyes.

"What happened to you Jake?" Johnny asked.

"I don't know," Jake said. "I think the bitch stole my money. I came up here pretty drunk and she helped me off with my things. Next thing I know she was gone and so are my pants."

Johnny looked around the room. Sure enough Jake's clothes were gone. Everything was missing except the underwear and boots he was still wearing.

Suddenly he heard Jake laugh. "There's one thing the bitch forgot," he said. "My diamond ring."

He fell sound asleep even as Johnny continued to try to rouse him. He was so busy shaking Jake that he did not hear the footsteps behind him until something heavy bashed his skull. As his knees wobbled, he caught a blurred glimpse of a woman holding the butt end of a gun and realized that Jake's girl had not forgotten about the ring. After that everything went black.

When he came to the morning sun was streaming through the windows and he could hear the heavy breathing of Jake Harkins on the bed.

His mouth felt as if it were full of cotton. His head felt as if someone had been beating it with a flat rock. Taking a last look at Jake's sleeping form, he left the room and made his way down the stairs. The place was empty. He heard some sounds coming from the kitchen but did not wait to find out who was making them.

As soon as he reached the street, he began walking briskly toward the marshall's office. There were few people abroad at that early hour. A lone Conestoga wagon was making its way down Front Street, obviously intent on making an early start West on the Santa Fe Trail. A couple of cowboys, obviously sleeping it off, were propped up against hitching rails.

When he reached Masterson's office, he remembered his warning about the place being watched and instead of stopping, merely passed by slowly. He saw Bat sitting against the wall through the window, obviously not seeing him. Taking a chance, he planted his face firmly against the glass, as if he were just peering curiously inside. It worked. Bat looked up at him and then waved his hand toward the Greene Hotel. Johnny went there at once and walked through the empty lobby. A moment later he was in his room.

Ten minutes after that, he heard a soft knock on his door and Bat Masterson closed it behind him.

"Sorry Bat," Johnny began. "I got hit by a bottle or something when I went back to the place. I came to just a little while ago."

Bat nodded grimly. "It's too late to worry about that now. I took a chance and sent one of my deputies to Larned. I hope he gets there in time. I wish to hell he was somewhere where we could telegraph him. Larned's just an old Indian fort with a small town near it. Anyway we can't depend on the deputy. He started pretty late and may not have caught Sherman who likes to get moving early I understand. We have to find out what's being set up at this end."

"How do we do that?" Johnny asked. "Through Lola?"

"No," Bat said. "She'll deny everything. Say you were drunk. Besides you heard her tell him not to reveal anything. The only thing she can tell us is who the man is. Then we can grab him."

"He may not be working alone."

"That's right," Bat agreed. "We may have to just watch his moves. But we can't do that unless we know who he is. It's no use my going to Lola. She'll swear up and down you lied. You heard her say she doesn't want any part of this. There's one way though if you're willing to work for us."

"Shoot," Johnny said.

"Go talk to her sister. If you fail I'll have a go at it. But I'd rather let you try first. She's liable to clam up if she thinks I'm trying to get Lola. Maybe if you tell her Lola's in a bad situation unless she tells us who this man is, she may persuade her to talk."

"If you think it'll help," Johnny said doubtfully.

"Johnny I can't guarantee anything," Bat said. "But I think it's worth a try."

He pulled a gold watch out of his vest pocket.

"She's just getting up now because she has to teach school. If you get to her room now, you may catch her in time. Her room's the second from the left end on this side. I'll be waiting here for you."

As Johnny closed the door behind him, he listened for sounds of any movement on the stairs. All was quiet. He moved cautiously down the carpeted corridor to the left end. As he reached Penny's room, he heard voices behind her door.

"I've got to leave Sam," she was saying. "If you're going to drive me to the school, we'd better go now. Besides I don't think it's right for you to be in my room this way. If Lola heard about it she'd be furious."

"I don't think so," Billings said. "She wants us to get married."

"I haven't agreed to marry you," Penny said carefully. "And I do not want to talk about it now. Please drive me to the school."

"Come here Penny. We can settle this once and for all," Billings said. "I knew we were going to be married the first time I saw you."

Johnny heard the sound of scuffling inside, then Penny's alarmed voice: "Please Sam, I don't want you to do that. Let me go."

"Damn it Penny, will you stop acting like a damn fool. It's about time you had a man. You're probably the only woman in this town who hasn't."

"Stop it," Penny yelled. "You're hurting me."

Johnny hesitated. The scuffle inside disturbed him but he preferred to speak to Penny without Billings knowing about it.

"You're tearing my dress," Penny screamed.

"Don't be a fool," Billings said sharply, "I'm not going to hurt you. Don't yell like that. You'll wake the whole neighborhood."

"Let me go," she screamed. She began to sob.

Johnny Blaise could stand no more. He stood back from the door and rammed against it with his shoulder. The door gave way under his bull-like rush and he entered the room.

He saw Penny Flynn lying on the bed, her dress torn down the middle, her bosom exposed, her long dark hair tumbled awry over her shoulders. Lying next to her with his arms around her was Sam Billings. The girl was fighting desperately to get away from him as he tried to pull her closer.

As the Texan leaped into the room, he pulled his gun from its holster and aimed it carefully at Billings.

"Get your hands off her," Johnny barked at him. "Get up fast."

Billings, obviously stunned by the cowboy's entry blinked and stared at him. Then he took his arms away from the sobbing girl and stood up.

"Hands high mister," Johnny ordered. With a quick movement, he reached over and pulled the Easterner's gun from its holster.

Penny Flynn reddened as she realized that her breast was exposed to the view of both men. She seized up the red calico bedspread and covered her bosom with it.

"You'll pay for this cowboy," Billings said. "I don't like people who interfere in private business."

"It sounded more like rape to me," Johnny said cooly.

"The lady and I are engaged," Billings said hotly.

"Since when do you have call to attack your fiancee?" Johnny asked. I could hear her screaming down the hall. Are you engaged to this man ma'am?"

Penny shook her head emphatically.

"Get going Mister," Johnny said. "I ought to run you into the Sheriff's office for attacking a woman, but I don't want to cause her any more trouble or embarrassment."

"Get out yourself and leave us alone." retorted Billings. "You're interrupting a private quarrel. The lady and I have a lot to talk about. And none of it is any business of yours."

Johnny looked quietly at Penny Flynn. "Do you want me to go and leave you alone ma'am? If you do, just say so and I'll go."

"No," Penny said nervously. "Don't leave me alone with him. I'm afraid. Can you drive me to the schoolhouse? It's not far."

"No trouble at all ma'am," Johnny said. "I can rent a horse and buggy nearby. I'll wait outside till you get properly dressed."

"Thank you," she said gratefully.

"You're out of your mind going with him," Billings said scornfully. "He'll probably take you to some tent on the prairie and force you to sleep with him there. You don't know these drunken cowboys. They attack Indian squaws, Mexican girls, lone women, anything in sight. You'll probably be turned over to his friends after he's through with you. Don't do it, Penny, I beg of you."

Penny looked worriedly at Johnny, obviously remembering his behavior toward her the night before. He caught the look of doubt and concern in her eyes.

"Don't worry about me ma'am," he said quietly. "Last night I was drunk and maybe a little impolite. But I could have done the same thing this "Eastern Gentleman"—he said the words contemptuously—"did if I had a mind to. There was nobody around last night and it was very dark. If that's what I wanted to do, I could have done anything and nobody would have heard your cries."

"That's true," she said thoughtfully. "You could have. Please wait outside Mr er ..."

"Blaise ma'am," he smiled. "Johnny's my Christian name."

"Lola won't like this when I tell her," Billings said angrily.

"She won't like it when I tell her you tried to attack me early in the morning by storming into my room," she said irritably in reply. She turned away from her and moved to her closets to seek a new dress.

Johnny motioned to Billings to move to the door. When the door was closed behind them, he said:

"Move fast Mister. I don't like you and this gun might go off."

"I won't forget this," Billings said ominously, as he left.

Johnny waited until he heard Billings' footsteps in the lobby below. Then he knocked quickly on Penny's door.

"Let me in please," he whispered through the door.

The girl opened the door a crack and he could see the growing fear in her eyes.

"I've got to talk to you privately," he said. He pushed aside the door and. closed it behind him.

The girl sprang back in alarm. She was wearing only her underclothes and a sleeveless garment which barely covered her full bosom. She cowered as he came closer.

"He was right," she said horrified. She seemed ready to scream.

Johnny blushed as he saw Penny's exquisite figure in the long white linen drawers with frilly embroidery on them and her mature breasts straining at her shift.

"No, no I'm sorry. I just had to get out of the hall that's all. I don't want to be seen."

He turned his back. "You can finish your dressing now. I won't look I promise."

"What do you want to talk about?" she said suspiciously, still not believing him. She pulled her dress over her head quickly.

"About your sister Lola," he said.

"Lola? What's Lola got to do with you?" she asked surprised.

"Not with me," Johnny said. "But she knows the man that's out to kill General William Sherman, and they're going to do it today."

"What did you say?" she said incredulously.

"Here. Today," he said quickly. "We have no time to lose. That's why I ran up here to see you. Looks like I timed my visit right too."

There was a long silence. Then Penny said: "If this is your idea of a joke I think it's in very bad taste."

"I'm not joking ma'am," he snapped. "Marshall Masterson is waiting down the hall to talk to you himself. I just learned about the plot a few hours ago and we need your help."

"I don't believe you," she said distraught. "You're drunk and you're using that as an excuse to come back here. You'd better leave immediately before I call the manager …"

"I'm not leaving till you hear me out …" he began.

"And I think it disgusting of you to charge my sister with anything like this."

"I'm not charging your sister with anything. Neither is the Marshall as far as I can make out. But if anything happens to General Sherman your sister will be involved. She knows the man behind the plot."

"I don't believe you," she said hotly. She was so angry she had stopped pulling her dress over her head. "If there were a shred of truth in your stupid story why didn't you go directly to Lola herself?"

"Because Masterson doesn't think she's willing to help stop this business. Listen Miss Flynn, why don't you finish dressing so I can turn around. I feel mighty silly talking with my back turned to you like this. And Marshall Masterson's waiting like I said."

"I'll be through in a moment," Penny said irritably. She was having difficulty pulling the dress over her hips.

"This dress is too small," she said out loud. "I told that silly woman to make it bigger at the hips."

"I'll be glad to help you," Johnny said, grinning.

"Keep your back turned if you don't mind," she said. "I still don't know whether to believe a word you're saying. My sister's told me all Texans are mad. Are you seriously trying to tell me there's a plot to kill General Sherman here today?"

CHAPTER SIX

"That's right, ma'am," he said quietly.

"Please turn around," she said after another moment. "I'm finished now."

Johnny turned and was shocked by the look on the girl's face. She sat down on a small upholstered chair and stared miserably at the floor.

"I can't believe Lola would do anything like that."

Johnny hesitated and said, "If you've got something to tell me about this. I'm listening. I may as well tell you I heard Lola discussing a plot to kill Sherman. I was in the next room, remember."

"You mean you were spying on us," Penny said angrily. "What are you, a Pinkerton man?"

He sighed. "I didn't say your sister is planning to kill him. But she knows who is," he said stubbornly. "Let me tell you what I heard."

He repeated what he had heard. She listened quietly, but he noted a growing uneasiness in her eyes as he continued.

"If there's anything you can tell me about the man," he said, "I'll be very grateful, ma'am. So will the Marshall."

Penny walked to the table near the bed and picked up a copy of the Dodge City newspaper. She read the story silently:

GENERAL WILLIAM T. SHERMAN TO
VISIT DODGE CITY TODAY

General William Tecumseh Sherman will spend the day in Dodge City today, arriving late this morning from Fort Larned.

The commanding general of the U. S. Army is making a tour of Army installations in Kansas, Missouri and Illinois.

After a tour of the area, General Sherman will confer with officers of Fort Dodge.

The remainder of the story detailed General Sherman's career during the war and afterwards. Penny had read the item in the paper in cursory fashion earlier but had not paid much attention.

"I still can't believe Lola would be involved in anything like this," she said stubbornly. "You must have been mistaken in what you heard."

She paused for a moment and then pursued this idea gratefully as if it offered a solution.

"That's it. I'm sure. You were probably drunk and sleepy and imagined you heard all this. You must have been drunk. I saw you drink all that strong whiskey myself."

"I'm sorry ma'am," Johnny said. "I may have been drunk when I went upstairs, but I wasn't drunk when I woke up. I can repeat almost word for word what went on between you and your sister."

He coughed delicately and said: "You were trying on some of Lola's underwear and she was mighty displeased with you about it. Also you told your sister you were unhappy about your—er—figure."

Penny blushed a deep red. Johnny looked uncomfortable.

"I'm sorry but I had to tell you to convince you I knew what was happening. I know how you feel. Lola's your sister and it's natural for you to defend her. All I know is what I heard from my own ears."

Penny was staring at the floor. She seemed to be speaking to herself. "I just can't believe Lola would be a party to anything so terrible," she said slowly." She hates Sherman because his men burned our house in Savannah. I was too young to remember it but my sister's told me a dozen times about it. They came with torches and set fire to the drapes. My mother died soon afterwards."

"I should think that was reason enough to want to kill Sherman," Johnny said. "But we still can't let it happen. Will you come and talk to Masterson please?"

She nodded in a stunned way, still trying to cope with what he had told her.

Bat Masterson greeted them quietly. "I'm sorry, ma'am," he said. But you may be able to help us, and like Mr. Blaise told you, there isn't much time. The General may be in Dodge City in a couple of hours."

"What do you want me to do?" she said listlessly.

"Tell us who the man was your sister was talking to last night."

She hesitated. "Are you going to arrest my sister?"

Masterson shook his head. "I'm not interested in your sister unless she's actively conspiring to kill the General. What Johnny here told me doesn't indicate she is. If I tried to round up every man or woman in Dodge who hated Sherman, I'd have to build a new jail. No, I'm not after Lola. But I have to ask you not to tell her we know about her conversation last night. She may not be conspiring against Sherman. But she may want to help the ones who are. We can't take chances."

Penny said nothing.

Who is Dabney, Miss Blaise?" Masterson asked carefully.

Penny hesitated and then said: "It's probably Dabney Anders. A grain dealer in Kansas City. I've met him once or twice."

"Tell us what you know about him please," Masterson said evenly.

"He's a former Confederate officer from Georgia," she said slowly. "He served with my brother and was with him when he died at Shiloh. When he heard my sister was out here he came to see her."

"What sort of dealings has he had with your sister?" Masterson asked.

"She's invested some money in his business I believe," Penny said. "I really don't know too much about him."

"What can you tell us that might help?" the Sheriff asked.

"He didn't strike me as the kind of person who would commit murder."

Masterson laughed politely. "Ma'am you'd be astonished how nice killers can be. Do you know where he might be staying here in Dodge?"

She shook her head. Then her face brightened. "The last time he was here he told me he didn't like staying in town, but liked to live outside. He used to drive in from some place nearby."

Masterson thought for a moment. "We can check on where he might be staying near town. Can you give us a full description of him ma'am? It would help a lot."

Penny described him as carefully as she could. "He was a tall, broad-shouldered man with blue eyes and red hair and spoke with a deep Southern drawl."

Masterson nodded. "Well it isn't much. But the red hair might help. Any special habits or clothes?"

Penny tried to remember.

"I'm sorry," she said helplessly. "I just can't think of anything."

"Never mind," Bat Masterson said. "We'll find him if he's here." He rose. "Why don't you take Miss Flynn to the schoolhouse now, Johnny? I've got to go talk to some people. You might drop by the office when you come back."

Johnny nodded. Bat Masterson said goodby to Penny and left hurriedly. A moment later Penny and Johnny were on their way out of the hotel. At the entrance, however, Penny turned back suddenly.

"Please wait here for me Mr. Blaise," she said.

"Please say Johnny," he said smiling.

"All right, Johnny. I won't be a minute." She turned to the stairs.

"Where are you going? You're not going to talk to Lola are you?"

She reddened.

He took her arm. "We'd better go Penny. You'll be late for school."

"I have to see her for a moment," she said. "I can't just go off like this. She may ...."

She did not finish but Johnny understood.

"She may try to help Dabney," he said quietly. "You're not too convinced she'll keep out of this, isn't that it?"

"She's such a hot-headed fool about the war and the Yankees," Penny said. "I'm afraid she may do something foolish not knowing what may happen. Please let me tell her at least to stay clear of Dabney. To have nothing to do with him."

"I can't let you do that Penny," Johnny said uncomfortably. "There's too much at stake."

"You think she's conspiring with the others," Penny said accusingly.

Johnny flushed. "I don't think anything. Let's get moving though."

Penny stood there defiantly. The Texan stared at her for a moment, uncertain what to say next. Suddenly he heard his name called.

Amos Greene hurried up to him.

"Mr. Blaise," he said nervously. "I wish you'd leave as soon as possible. I don't want shooting here."

"What shooting?" Johnny asked surprised.

"Well a little while ago I saw Billings come through here madder than hell. Said he was going to get a gun and come back and teach you a lesson. Wanted me to tell him if you were still upstairs or where you'd gone if you weren't."

Johnny smiled. "Well now ain't that nice of him."

Suddenly a thought occurred to him. "Maybe I'll wait for him right here. Miss Flynn ain't in no hurry to get to school."

"I wouldn't if I was you Mr. Blaise," Greene said. "Billings is a pretty good shot. He killed someone a week ago in a poker fight."

"Don't scare me none," Johnny said. He pulled his gun from its holster and examined it carefully to see if it was half-cocked. It was.

"Please make him go Miss Flynn," Greene begged. "I don't want any killing in here."

Penny looked at Johnny and made up her mind. "I think we'd better leave Johnny. Mr. Greene's right."

"What? Me run away from a fight?" Johnny said in mock astonishment. "No sirree. I'll wait for Mr. Tenderfoot right here."

"He ain't no ordinary tenderfoot," Greene expostulated. "He's a dead shot I tell you and he's killed a man. A few yards from here."

"Please come," Penny said, pleadingly.

"Okay," Johnny said finally. "Let's go."

He turned to Greene. "You tell Mr. Billings I'll be glad to oblige him anywhere and anytime. And in case he thinks he's undermatched tell him I've been hitting bulls eyes for a long time."

He grinned and walked out with Penny. She looked at him with undisguised respect.

"I've heard that you Texans were a little wild and ready to take up any challenge," she said. "But I'd better warn you that Billings hasn't been challenged by anybody since I've been here. He has a reputation for being too fast on the draw."

Johnny grinned. "That so? Well that ought to make it real interesting then. We'd better hurry us over to that school now."

He saw no sign of Billings on the road to the schoolhouse, which lay about a mile behind the town near the river. Penny watched the horizon nervously as if she expected Billings to come charging on them with his gun blazing. They passed rows of tents and corrals filled with cattle waiting to be shipped east. Several cowboys waved to them.

At the schoolhouse, where a dozen children were waiting, she turned to him and said: "You will be careful won't you?"

"I'm always careful, Penny," he answered. He looked at her pupils. Three of them were wearing holsters and guns.

"Say teaching seems mighty dangerous around here. You allow those kids to come to school armed? Maybe I ought to stick around to protect you."

She smiled. "It was a shock the first time I saw them with guns, but I'm used to them now. Do be careful."

He waved as he rode off back to town. To be on the safe side, just in case Billings was aiming at some surprise, he took another path back to town. He passed several more corrals filled with milling cattle, encampments of Conestoga wagons and new tent communities. The outskirts of Dodge seemed full of people on the move as the big wagons began rolling. He waved affably to the wagon men.

He thought he knew everything in the neighborhood of Dodge, but he failed to recognize the house that appeared before him now. It was a small place, screened from the road by a copse of trees. He looked at it with interest and was wondering who lived in it, when a voice called his name. Turning around, he saw Frenchy, the girl from the "line," in the doorway. Her lush curves were barely covered by a robe.

"Hallo. Don't you recognize me Johnny?" she said warmly. "Did you come out to see me?"

He blinked. He had forgotten all about her.

"Well not this time Frenchy," he said hurriedly, stopping the horse and buggy near the door. "Maybe I can come back later though." The dark-eyed girl's loveliness was enhanced by her loose robe which revealed the upper portion of her full breasts.

"But of course," she said pleased. "You can stay here too. I have one room free." She let the robe open slightly.

He grinned. "You taking in boarders?"

"Oui. Only friends. There is a man from Chicago and one from Kansas City. I charge them a little more than the hotel in Dodge, but they prefer to stay with me." He could see her breasts now. Their fullness and the dark aureoles in their center.

She smiled. "Can you blame them cherie?"

Johnny looked at her voluptuous figure and shook his head.

"Not a bit. Hell I'm beginning to be sorry I put up at the hotel, myself."

"Come in for a moment darling," she said. "And have some coffee."

He felt tempted to stay. The look on Frenchy's face was open invitation. No doubt of it.

"Please stay," she said, leading him into the airy kitchen. "My guests are not here and we can be alone all morning."

"I'd love to Frenchy," he said, "But I can't. Not today."

A man would have to be made of wood not to want to stay, he thought. But he had to get back to town to help Masterson locate Dabney Anders. He shook his head sadly.

"But I do not wish to charge you for keeping me company," she said, misunderstanding his motive in refusing. "I am inviting you cherie. And I will make some lunch for us later."

"Please don't insist lady," he said. "I really have urgent business in Dodge. It ain't the money. Whatever you charge, you're worth it. Every dollar."

She sighed. "Why is it I have to like always a crazy vaquero? A woman offers herself for nothing and he turns away."

She let her loose robe open completely. He looked at her and blinked. She was wearing nothing underneath. In the bright morning sun, her supple olive-skinned thighs and hips and the exquisitely wrought globes of her breasts glistened with magic. Quickly she threw her arms around him and drew him close.

He became a little dizzy with the heady scent of her young and beautiful body. The hardness of her breasts against him almost made him forget where he was.

"Would you like to help me take my bath," she said mischievously.

"Frenchy, ordinarily I'd give my eye tooth to help you take your bath," he said, "but today I just got to get back to town. There's something important I got to attend to."

"What in heaven's name is so important in town that everyone has to leave like this," she said grumpily. "The one from Kansas City too—jumped out of bed and was gone almost before he finished shaving."

Kansas City, he thought. The man was from Kansas City. The name struck a chord. Could it possibly be Anders? Why not, he thought. Penny had said he was staying on the edge of town. And he had come from Kansas City. He would have to be careful in asking questions however. There was no need to arouse the girl's suspicions or give her anything to pass on to Anders.

He rubbed his chin. "I think I can manage to stay a little while. Do you think I could take a shave while you take your bath, honey. I was going to do that in my room, but I won't have time if I stay here."

"Ah, oui," Frenchy said delighted. "Come, I show you where my guest has his things."

She led him into another room and showed where the guest ad left his razor and towel. He looked carefully at the razor and the washstand. He could see nothing as yet. He kissed Frenchy and began to smear his face with soap. Frenchy laughed and then went into another room. As soon as she had left, he examined the stand and the floor more carefully. There were a few black hairs. He rose disappointed but a moment later he brightened as a thought occurred to him.

"Frenchy, is there another razor?" he called out. "This one needs sharpening."

"In the room to the right," she called. "When you are finished come in to the left. You must scrub me in the back where I
cannot reach, mon chou."

He moved quickly to the next room. His eyes widened as
soon as he reached the washstand. There on the stand and on
the towel were red hairs. He examined the room quickly. There
were no books or papers around that could tell him anything. He
would have to confirm his guess through Frenchy.

When he entered her room, the dark-skinned girl was sprin-
kling some powder into a tub. It was big enough for someone to
sit in, that was all. As he entered, Frenchy cast off her robe and
said to him: "Please hold the sides while I go inside"

Johnny scared at the contraption in amazement. He had
never seen anything like it before.

"Where in hell's name did you get that?" he asked.

"A girl from New Orleans bought it from Lotta Crabtree the
beautiful actress when she came to Dodge. Now I bought it from
her. Please soap my back, mon ami. But easily, or my skin will be
hurt."

He took the soap and made it lather in his hands. Then he
moved his fingers over her magnificent body. She sighed as his
fingers kneaded the soft flesh of her back.

"Aye aye aye!" she said. "You have magic in those fingers. You
should do this to every woman you know."

He waited a moment, until he had lulled her into a state of
drowsy delight with his caressing fingers and the white soap had
streaked onto her glistening thighs, smooth, flat belly and firm,
full breasts. Then he said very casually.

"Who is your friend with the red hair?"

"Why?" she asked slyly. "You are jealous?"

"Yes," he lied. "Very jealous. The razor looks familiar. I knew
someone who used that kind of razor. It would not be a tall,
strong man from the South for example?"

"Aha you are jealous," she laughed. "Please, more soap on my back cherie. What is his name?"

"Anders, Dabney Anders. A former Confederate officer."

"Wrong. This one is Henry Thompson. However he too was in the Rebel Army."

Frenchy yawned. "Your hands make me feel so sleepy. I think I would like to lie down in my bed. Will you come and keep me company, M'sieu Texas."

She reached out for the towel beside her and then standing up, presented her lovely body for his admiration.

"Won't Mr. Thompson be coming back?" he asked.

"Oh yes, but not for some hours," she said. "We have much time."

"When do you think he'll come?" he persisted. "We could be disturbed."

Her eyes looked surprised. "I think not before noon. The other man won't be back till evening. Or don't you care about him?" she added slyly. He flushed at her tone.

"Sure I do," Johnny said, running his fingers mischievously along her smooth thighs.

She threw her arms about him and drew his face down to her clean, sweet smelling flesh. "Don't lie to me mon chou," she said smiling. "I like you very much, but you are a very very poor actor. I do not believe anything you say about razors or old friends. Admit that you are looking for someone who is staying with me."

He hesitated.

"Perhaps you would prefer to have me tell him you were asking then? His old friend?" she said, her eyes twinkling.

She sat down on the bed and began to paint her toe nails with a small brush. When she had finished, she examined her work.

"A girl from New Orleans taught me this," she said playfully. She lifted a beautifully-turned leg high in the air to dry the paint, then slyly tickled his nose with her big toe. He grasped her bare foot—it was tiny and seemed more like a child's than a woman's. He kissed the toe.

"So I shall tell M'sieu Thompson that his friend is looking for a Mr. Anders?" she asked mischievously. "Perhaps I can even tell him where you can be found. Oui?"

She twirled her other bare leg in the air. The drops of water on the coffee-colored thigh glistened like sequins in the sun. He sighed, kissed her instep and decided that he had to trust her. She was a prostitute, but that did not matter. He had to make a decision.

"I must trust you, little one," he said slowly. "Somehow I do not think you will let me down. I like you very much and I trust my liking."

Her eyes watched him with a shrewdness that told him she had known all the time there was something going on. He told her about the plot to assassinate General Sherman and his search for the red-headed ex-Confederate officer.

She listened very quietly. At the end she said: "I do not like assassin. I do not know this General of yours. But I do not like killing a man because he fought well, because he was a good soldier. My father was killed by the Mexicans for that. He was an officer in Maximilian's army. When the French were defeated, they executed him. He had done nothing but fight as a good soldier is supposed to. They blamed him for the death of hundreds of Mexicans, for what happened to their homes."

"Then you will help us," he said hopefully.

"Oui, oui," she said. "But you must tell me how. What I must do."

"You must give us a signal when he arrives. I will be watching for it. Make a small fire. Use any excuse so that the smoke will rise. That will tell us he is here. If you learn anything else of interest and want to communicate with us, it's better that you come to the Marshall's office at once."

"I will do it," she said quickly.

"But be careful," he warned. "If he's the man I think he is, he won't hesitate to kill you. Promise me to be careful."

"I promise," she said. She kissed him quickly. "You were not joking when you said you liked me?"

"No," he said. "Now I must hurry back to the Sheriff. He is waiting for me in Dodge City."

As he rose to leave they heard the sound of a rider approaching. She looked frightenedly through the window. In the distance she saw a cloud of dust speeding toward the house. He would be there in a moment. She recognized the rider and turned to Johnny.

"It's Monsieur Harrigan," she said, "the other guest. He and Thompson are good friends."

"I'd better go," Johnny said quickly. "I don't want him to know I'm here."

"It's too late," she said. "He will see you. Come here and take off your things."

"Take off my things?" he said skeptically. "What for?"

She shut the door and drew back the coverlet from her bed. "If he sees a man in bed with me, he will not be suspicious. Quick, mon cher, he will be here in a moment."

Johnny stood there paralyzed for a few seconds, then he began to undress with feverish haste. He had some difficulty pulling off his boots and she helped him. In no time at all, he had piled his duds in a pyramid on the floor and plunged under the coverlet with Frenchy. She put her arms around him and pulled him sharply to her freshly-bathed skin. He was too concerned with the arrival of the newcomer to react to the girl for a moment. But he was too human not to react after that moment.

As he felt the girl's body tremble against his own and the sharp peaks of her firm breasts like knives against his chest, his temples began to pound and he found himself growing more nervous every instant. A moment later she sighed as she felt a change coming over him and she began to writhe against him, moaning in French.

His hands began to roam over Frenchy's mare-like thighs and her smooth flat belly. The electric shock of his fingertips made her cry out and forced him to stop her mouth with his hand.

"That you Frenchy?" he heard a deep voice ask from the next room. Johnny removed his hand from her lips.

"Oui," she said out loud.

Suddenly Johnny saw the door open slightly. Frenchy pushed his face against her so the new arrival could not make out his features.

"Well I'm sorry to interrupt," the man said amiably. "One of my regular clients," she said brusquely. "He was passing by and came to see me. Please close the door amigo." "Sure, sure," the man said, his eyes surveying the other man's head and his piled up clothes with amusement. "You go right ahead. Sorry I interrupted Mister," he yelled to Johnny. He shut the door quickly behind him.

"I'd better go," Johnny whispered a moment later. "Maybe I can leave through the back way."

"No yet," she cautioned. "He'll be suspicious. Wait at least ten or fifteen minutes. Besides," she added grumpily, "you have picked a fine time to go. I thought you said you liked me."

He sighed, took her in his arms and kissed her warmly. He could not erase the image of Penny Flynn from his mind, but he was only human. It was impossible to lie in bed with a beautiful girl and pretend you were an iceberg. He wanted her badly and now there was no sense in fooling himself. Since he couldn't leave anyway, it was crazy holding back, he thought.

He kissed her again, tenderly at first, then with a savage, demanding passion. His hands roamed excitedly over her warm, clean body as it twisted nimbly under his touches. In a few moments, his caresses had become unbearable to the girl and she was almost ready to jump out of her skin. The sharp points of her breasts, the supple flesh of her legs and thighs and the rich scent of her freshly-soaped body made him feel as if he had left the ground and was soaring high in the air. Before long, as they lay clasped in each other's arms, both their bodies were wet with perspiration.

When it was all over, they lay back, exhausted, yet happy, aware of the strength and the wonder of their bodies.

"I'll be going to town to get my mail in a minute Frenchy. Anything you want honey?" The man in the next room said loudly, breaking into their calmness.

"No thank you," Frenchy said at last when she found her voice.

"Okay. I think Thompson should be along soon. Sure you don't want nothing now?"

"No," Frenchy said. She kissed Johnny's bare shoulder. "I don't want anything." She laughed and said softly to Johnny: "We can be alone now mon chou. No one will bother us."

To her chagrin and astonishment, the Texan jumped out of bed as soon as he heard the girl's boarder slam the door to the street. He waited for the sound of his horse's hooves to make sure he had really left and then began to dress quickly.

"Where are you going?" Frenchy cried angrily. "You can't just run away like this."

"Sorry Frenchy," Johnny said. "I've got to get back to town or there'll be hell to pay."

She stared at him open-mouthed as he shut the door behind him and ran toward his horse.

CHAPTER SEVEN

As the sun reached its zenith the stage coach and its military escort reached the top of the hill. Down below, shimmering faintly in the dusty sunlight like some mirage lay the saloons, dance halls and hotels of Dodge City. Beyond it stretched the meandering ribbon of the Arkansas River. The lieutenant in charge of the six-man escort dismounted and opened the door of the coach. A moment later a tall, spare man in uniform stepped out and jumped gingerly to the ground. His blue eyes took the scene in quickly. Without looking behind him he held out his hand. An aide de camp quickly handed him a pair of binoculars. The tall man put them up to his eyes and studied the buildings far down on the plains.

"Mmn!" he said. "So that's the wildest cow town in the country. Doesn't look like much. Looks more like some little quiet place in the middle of nowhere."

Looks are deceiving General," the lieutenant said. "I can assure you that plenty goes on day and night. When we get a bit closer you'll probably be able to hear their six shooters. When they get drunk, which is most of the time, they like a lot of noise."

The aide-de-camp coughed delicately.

"What is it captain!" General Sherman growled. "Whenever I hear that damned cough of yours I know you're itching to say something. Well spit it out man! Don't they teach you to talk at the academy these days?"

"Yes sir," the captain said. "I merely wished to suggest that it might be better for us to have lunch at Fort Dodge with the commandant instead of in Dodge City itself."

General Sherman shook his head and turned to the lieutenant. "He's afraid some Johnny Reb might try to put a bullet through me."

"Sir, the man who gave us the message at Larned said there was a plot to kill you."

"I heard him," Sherman retorted. "There have been rumors of such plots ever since the war ended. Nothing's ever happened. Nothing ever will happen. Soldiers respect one another."

"Why not give the Sheriff a chance to learn who's behind the plot sir?" the captain said. "We could spend the night at Fort Dodge and in the morning..."

"No," Sherman said with finality. "I'm not going to hide behind a damned stockade like some lily-livered civilian. I'm a general of the United States Army. You told me Dodge is full of former Rebel officers. Then that's one reason more for me not to hide."

The captain began to say something else, but the expression on Sherman's face stopped him.

"Let's go," Sherman said a moment later. "I'm anxious to see what the so-called Sodom of the Prairie looks like." A smile grew on his face. "If you're worried Captain, you have my permission to ride off to the fort. You can pick me up tomorrow morning when we're ready to leave."

The stagecoach proceeded down the hill until it reached the outskirts of town where it was met by a group of horsemen. One of them stepped down and moved up to the coach. He put his head in the doorway.

"My name is Bat Masterson sir," he said. "I'm the Marshall here. Welcome to Dodge City, General."

"Thank you," Sherman said. "Now I hope you're not going to make a big fuss about this visit. I'm just passing through."

"Yes sir. We just came out to meet you a little ways to make sure everything was all right."

"You came out to see if a pack of malcontents were going to kidnap me," the General snapped good-naturedly. "Let's not mince words Masterson."

"Okay General," Masterson said grinning. "Well you're a pretty important visitor to these parts and we don't want anything to go wrong. I take it nothing happened along the road then."

"Yes, I breathed in a ton of Kansas dust," Sherman said. "But I'm used to it. I was stationed at Leavenworth before the war. Can we move on, I'm a little tired. I'd rather sit eight hours on a spavined horse than ride through Kansas in a stagecoach."

"Yes sir," Masterson said. "Well take you right to the hotel. The Mayor's got a little reception ready for you there. We'll have a group of deputies around the entrance to see nothing interferes."

"Marshall if that means you're going to keep Confederate soldiers away from me, change your plan. I want to be accessible to any veteran who wants to talk to me. Union or Confederate. Is that clear?"

"Well yes, General," Masterson said uncomfortably, "but there are a lot of hot-heads in Dodge. Didn't you talk to the man I sent out to meet your party?"

"I did," the General said, "and my decision still stands. I am ready to talk to any former fighting man who wants to see me."

"Yes sir," Masterson said. He moved away, mounted his horse and waved to the stage driver to follow him. As they began to roll toward town, he turned to a deputy riding beside him:

"No wonder he won so many fights," he said shaking his head. "I don't think the man knows fear."

A moment later he added: "But that ain't going to make our job easier. I wish young Blaise would get back."

As the stagecoach and its accompanying riders entered the town, the streets were lined with men and women staring with curiosity at the legendary hero of the Civil War. Many of them began to cheer wildly as the carriage passed and mothers held up small children to look. The General put his head out of the window and waved at the crowd. His complete unconcern about danger made Bat Masterson wince. The Marshall and his deputies looked carefully into the saloons and restaurants on Front Street to see if any guns were pointed.

Suddenly their horses reared as several guns began to fire at once. Masterson drew his gun and his eyes raked the crowd on both sides. He saw a half-dozen cowboys with their smoking guns pointed in the air leaning against hitchrails in the street. The General grinned at them.

Masterson stared at him nervously and wished he would put his head back in the coach.

Suddenly his deputy pointed to someone further down.

"There's a man waving at us down the road," he said. Bat Masterson looked at the waver. It was Johnny Blaise and he was pointing to the Marshall's office.

Masterson nodded quickly. He turned to his deputy. "I'm going to leave as soon as we reach the hotel. You stay with the General's party until further orders."

A moment later, he cut out and headed for his office. He was very anxious to know what Blaise had discovered.

A few minutes later he strode into his office. Shutting the door carefully, he turned to Johnny.

"Well what the hell happened to you. Did you stay for school or what? Sherman's ready to start his tour and we still don't have a clue about what's going on."

Johnny blushed and told him what he had learned at Frenchy's place, discreetly omitting his unscheduled bedroom scene with the Latin girl. He was pleased to see that Masterson was impressed. The Sheriff stood up and rubbed the handles of his guns.

"It may be just the man we're looking for. You better go out there as close to the place as possible. The minute you spot the signal, ride back to town. It isn't far to Frenchy's place."

"Right," Johnny said.

Bat Masterson looked at his watch. "I've got to get back to the Mayor's reception. After lunch the General's going to visit a few saloons and talk to people then he'll go out to the school house and talk to the kids. I wish to heaven he'd stick to the kids. There may be trouble at the drinking places. There's nothing more ornery than a drunken cowboy."

At the door, he turned and said: "You're a good man, Blaise. I'm sure you don't care much for Sherman. I never met a Texan who did. It's nice of you to go to all this trouble. I wish there were more like you around. Men who think of acting like citizens sometime instead of just drinking and whoring around."

Johnny reddened. "I guess I'd better move along," he said awkwardly.

"Fine," Masterson said. "Just keep in mind what the General's schedule is so you can act accordingly. That way if you see Anders or some gunmen leaving Frenchy's house you can figure where they're headed and try to get there first. Just to make sure I'm sending a few deputies to cover the south side of Frenchy's place. You better take the north side. Maybe we'll box them in that way. That is if Anders and his men are planning to use Frenchy's as a base. They may never go near the place."

"That's true," Johnny said. "She has no guarantee he'll show up."

"Okay," Masterson said. "General Sherman will be lunching at the Western Hotel with me and Mayor Kelly in half an hour. Then he'll kind of hold court in the lobby for an hour. Around two he'll inspect the cattle pens and the Santa Fe depot. Then he'll visit a few saloons. Oh, and before he gets to the saloons he'll make a little speech about the war to the kids at school."

The Sheriff sighed. "I'd better get back before old Kelly drinks up all that champagne he's saved in Uncle Billy's honor. I don't get much chance to taste champagne. I hope I don't have to drink it with one eye on my gun."

Johnny laughed. "Don't be so sure there'll be trouble. Could be Anders was bluffing."

Bat Masterson shook his head. "I don't think so. I did a little checking on Anders. If that's his real name, he's a bad hombre. He joined up with part of the old Quantrill gang after the war and he was in on some of their worst raids. Anyway no matter what happens I'm bound to be nervous with a man like Uncle Billy Sherman around. Too many Confederates, including some from Georgia. And if that's not enough, there are drunken cowboys, horsethieves and even whiskey-loco Indians."

"Indians?" Johnny said. "I thought the Cheyennes were living peacefully on their reservations."

"The Southern Cheyennes are. But their cousins from up north who were sent down here after Custer was wiped out at Big Horn aren't too happy. They hate the plains and the Kansas climate. Sometimes a pack of them go on a rampage and burn down some wagons on the Santa Fe trail. Or else a drunken warrior comes through with a Buffalo rifle. One of those Big Fifties that blows a man's head off."

He scratched his head. "That reminds me. You be extra careful on the road. The Indian bucks who make trouble usually wait till soneone's out of the town limits and those Cheyennes can move awful quietly."

CHAPTER EIGHT

Johnny decided his best observation point would be Penny's schoolhouse It was close enough to Frenchy's to see a smoke signal and he would not have to wait out in the open where he would be conspicuous. Besides, he told himself, he'd have the pleasure of seeing Penny Flynn again. He hoped his unexpected visit would not disturb her too much.

To his delight, it did not disturb her at all. If anything she seemed eager to see his face at the window. As soon as she could she came outside to speak to him.

"I can't do a thing with them. They're all agog about Uncle Billy Sherman's visit to the school. Some of them have even brought stories of his big victories for him to sign."

After a while he moved behind the school building, rolled himself a smoke and began to watch for a signal from Frenchy. For a long time nothing came. He contented himself with watching Penny give the kids their geography lesson and admiring her lovely face as she spoke. His curiosity and obvious interest embarrassed her a little and more than once she blushed as she caught his smile.

On his part, he decided he had never seen anyone so lovely in all his life. He was wondering how she would like to live on a ranch in Texas and how Tom would like her when he saw the first coil of smoke rising above Frenchy's chimney, half a mile away. He could not see the house too well because it was on a rise.

Instantly he waved goodby to Penny and mounting his horse, rode quickly toward the town. To his amazement he saw

Frenchy running out of her house and waving excitedly to him as he approached.

Bringing his mount to a halt, he waited for the breathless girl to speak.

"No. There is no time cherie. I heard him tell the other man they will meet Sherman at the schoolhouse. He is due there in ten minutes. I made the signal as soon as they left the house."

"The schoolhouse," he said amazed. "Are you sure?"

"I am sure. They thought I was asleep. But I heard them say it clearly. Everything is arranged for Sherman when he reaches the school."

"Did you hear anything else?"

Frenchy shook her head.

"You'd better get back to the house then" Johnny said. "And thank you."

"When will I see you again?"

He hesitated. "Soon I hope. Frenchy," he began, "I want to explain …"

She put her finger to his lips. "Not now mon couer. Now you must go try to save the General."

He sighed with relief. After all she had risked to help him, he felt he had to tell her how he felt about Penny. He was glad she had stopped him however. It wasn't easy telling a girl you had just made love to that you wanted to marry someone else.

He watched her retreating figure move toward the house and then mounted again. He had to reach the schoolhouse as soon as possible. He looked in vain for a sign of the deputy sheriff's. There was no sign of them. They were probably hiding in the woods that rose behind Frenchy's house. There was no time to warn them now.

By spurring his mount, he was able to reach the school quickly. Penny, who had been finishing her short account of General Sherman's life before his visit, was astonished to see him so soon. The children, equally surprised, began to giggle as soon as they recognized him.

He waved to her to come outside as soon as she could. She joined him a moment later. Quickly he told her what he must do. She thought for a few seconds, then her face reddened.

"There is one place you can hide in that has a perfect view of the house," she said embarrassedly.

"Where is it. I've go to get there fast," he said.

"The privy," she said, coloring again. "It's just a few yards away and you can see everything in the school from it as well as the surrounding terrain."

He squeezed her hand warmly and moved to the privy quickly.

When he was inside he surveyed the enclosure carefully. There were chinks high up in the wooden structure big enough for him to see through and even to put his gun barrel through. It was a perfect observation post, he thought elated. Not the most elegant perhaps, not the healthiest or the most pleasant, but probably the safest. He readied himself for a long wait. The General might be late and he might be in the school for an hour for all he knew.

Meanwhile he trained his eyes on the terrain. On one side of the schoolhouse was the flat plain leading to Dodge. On the other was a thickly wooded hill. If Anders and his killers were hiding anywhere, he decided it was probably in those woods. He scrutinized the hill carefully but could see nothing suspicious.

He did not have much time to study it. He was there less than fifteen minutes when he saw General Sherman's party ride up to the school. The hero of the battle of Atlanta dismissed his escorts a moment later when Penny came out to welcome him. Johnny saw Bat Masterson draw back to one side of the building while Sherman went inside, removed his hat and began speaking to the assembled children.

For what seemed an eternity nothing happened. Johnny watched the rapt faces of the children as they listened to the Civil War leader. Perhaps thirty yards away the accompanying soldiers and Dodge City dignitaries were busy chatting. He was almost convinced that nothing would happen when his eyes spotted a figure moving slowly down the hillside behind the school building. He had not noticed the figure moving through the scrub because it had been crouched. Now it stood up and he could see the rifle in its hands.

The rifle was pointed directly at the window where General Sherman stood sharply outlined, a perfect target. There was no time to warn him or anyone else. Aiming carefully, Johnny leveled his gun at the rifleman and fired. The figure dropped a second later. As if the shot had been a signal, several other figures rose from the scrub behind the fallen man and leveled guns at the schoolhouse. Johnny ran out of the house and began firing at them. The moment's respite had been enough to galvanize the soldiers and the Marshall's men into action.

Suddenly the hillside was raked by a barrage of gunfire from below. Moving closer to the hill, Johnny recognized the raiders as Indians. The redskins began retreating toward the crest of the hill, firing as they moved. Casting a quick glance at the schoolhouse to confirm that Sherman had not been hit, Johnny ran to his horse and moved after them. Behind him he could hear the angry shouts of men running to their horses and of children yelling wildly.

He fired at the retreating horsemen as he sped down the hill and noticed for the first time that there were white men with them. As he dropped two of the white raiders, firing from horseback, he saw Bat Masterson leading a group of riders from the other side of the killers. The raiders seeing themselves outflanked began to fire at both sides.

It was over a few moments later. There was no cover on the naked prairie once they were away from the wooded hillside and the raiders were outnumbered. After several of them had been wounded, the others obeyed Masterson's orders, dropped their guns and surrendered.

Bat Masterson rode over to Johnny and thanked him.

"That was pretty good shooting Johnny," he said admiringly.

Johnny laughed, "Maybe. But I'm sure glad you were along to help."

Soon afterwards the head of the military escort rode up and said that General Sherman wanted to thank the man who had saved his life. Johnny went to meet him at the schoolhouse and blushed as Penny and the school kids watched Sherman shaking his hand. He was pleased, nevertheless, with the admiration in Penny Flynn's eyes.

He had only a moment to speak to her but it was enough to ask if he could see her that night.

Her eyes shone. "I'd like that very much."

He promised to come for her as soon as he could. A moment later Masterson pulled him away and told him that Sherman insisted that he accompany the party and have dinner with them later.

"One of the men you hit was Anders," the Sheriff told him, as they rode back toward the town. "They had paid a few disgruntled Cheyennes to kill Uncle Billy. Beside giving them money they played on the Cheyennes' bitterness toward the soldiers for kicking them out of their hunting lands up north. The scheme was to make the killing look like it was done by a pack of wild drunken bucks full of hate and piss. And they might just have succeeded if you hadn't drawn a gun first. Nobody ever dreamed they'd pull anything at the schoolhouse."

It was impossible to get away from the visitors afterwards. General Sherman himself said he wanted the young cowboy to ride beside him, and tour the nearby fort.

When he saw he was not going to get away Johnny shyly asked the General's aide if he could bring Penny to the banquet in Sherman's honor. The General was delighted with the idea.

"The young man and his lady are my personal guests the rest of the evening," Sherman said laughing. "Besides I may need his protection."

He insisted that Penny and Johnny sit beside him at dinner and constantly refilled their glasses with champagne. To the assembled scores of diners and saloon owners, he described Johnny as one of the best shots he had ever met. He added, chuckling:

"Lord knows what might have happened if we'd run into marksmen like him at Shiloh or Atlanta."

The sally drew loud laughter from everybody present except two diners. The exceptions were Sam Billings and Lola Flynn who stared stonily at the Union leader. At the mention of Blaise's feat, Lola's face flushed with anger. She continued to stare moodily as the cowboy and her sister held hands and exposed their enchantment to everyone present.

"If that cowboy hangs around much longer," Billings said sourly, "I might as well go back to Chicago. Penny'll never marry me. She'll go back to Texas with the fool."

Lola's eyes blazed with anger. "Are you crazy? My sister marry a dumb Texas cowhand? A lariat swinger stinking of trail dust and sweat, a man barely able to read or write? You don't think a girl born and bred in an educated family will pass up an attorney educated in the East for a cowboy?"

Billings shook his head. "I saw them together. They don't even know people are around I tell you. All she does is moon at him Lola. The only way I have any chance is if the bastard leaves town."

"She's just being nice to him because Sherman's here," Lola insisted. "If I had my way I'd slit his throat for ruining Anders' scheme to kill that Yankee murderer. Don't fret Sam, Penny's as likely to marry that clod as I have of marrying the king of England."

A few days later she admitted she really was worried, however. At every free moment, Penny seemed ready to do anything Blaise wanted. She dined with him, danced with him and attended performances of a visiting theatrical troupe. When the Firemen had their regular ball, she went as his partner. During the long lazy afternoons Johnny would take her along the Arkansas River in a hired buckboard.

One day she came to Lola with excitement in her eyes and in a breathless voice told her that Johnny had proposed to her.

"I hope you said no," Lola said astonished.

"I'm not sure," Penny said. "I told him I'd give him my answer by the end of the week. He's planning to leave then for Texas."

"You'd be crazy to marry a cowboy, an illiterate fool who will be herding cows all his life when you have a fine man like Billings waiting for you."

Penny reddened. "I'm not in love with Sam Billings," she said "and I think I'm falling in love with John Blaise. Oh Lola you don't even know him. He's not illiterate. He had good schooling and he knows something about music and literature. He's even traveled with his brother and parents. And he's not just a cowhand. He owns a ranch in Texas and he has plans to expand it."

"He's just an ignorant cowhand," Lola stormed. "I've been in Dodge long enough to know them all. They're all filthy and ignorant. The moment they come to town they get stinking drunk and sleep with every whore in the cribs."

"Why do you accept their custom then?" Penny angrily countered. "I don't notice you shutting your doors to them."

"I accept it because I'm a businesswoman. As soon as I make enough money I'm going back to Chicago to buy real estate and live decently. Billings and I have big plans about that."

"I see," Penny said seriously. "And I'm part of them. You'd have me marry a man I don't love just so you can wrap up your plans neatly in a ribbon."

"You said you liked Billings, Penny," Lola said. "Maybe he's a little arrogant sometimes, but he's a man and he means well. He'll make you very happy. Blaise will make you miserable. He'll be tumbling every little Mexican bitch in Texas into the haystack the minute he gets you back there."

"He's not that kind of man," Penny said firmly. "Stop trying to run him down. He's sweet and kind and ..."

"And he's slept with half the dance hall girls in Dodge as well as some whores who couldn't even work in a dance hall because they're diseased. I can get you witnesses who saw him with girls on this trip and the last one."

"I don't believe you," Penny snapped. "And if he did go with such women it's all over. I don't expect men out here to act like monks. But he's incapable of anything like that now."

Lola eyed her sister shrewdly. If proof was what Penny needed to open her eyes about Blaise's whoring, that could be arranged without too much trouble. She was sure the Texan was as lecherous as the rest of his kind, always ready to bounce into bed with a willing wench and a bottle of whiskey. That could easily be arranged if she just had a little time.

"I won't stand in your way Penny," she said meekly now. "But as your older sister I think I have the right to ask you to be careful about a thing as important as this. Promise me you won't give him a definite answer for a week at least."

Penny hesitated.

"If you do that I'll come to the wedding and treat him as if he were someone I had picked myself," Lola said. "Otherwise I don't intend to have anything to do with either of you. I think you owe me that much consideration at least."

"But why should I wait that long?" Penny said, "He's leaving in three or four days. And I promised to let him know by then."

"If he loves you he'll wait gladly," Lola said smiling. "Learn not to give in too easily, my dear. It's for your own good."

That night she asked Olive Gomez to come to her room.

"Sit down Olive," she said affably. "I've got a little chore for you that I think you're going to like very much. And it'll pay well too."

"Fine," Olive said, her dark eyes flashing. "What is it?"

"Do you think you could make Johnny Blaise make love to you?"

Olive's eyes grew sullen. "That pig! Why should I get into bed with him."

"Never mind that!" Lola said impatiently. "But could you?"

"Si, si. But why should I? Besides he is crazy about your sister I hear" Olive said. Then she smiled understandingly. "I see. It will be a pleasure Lola. Don't worry about it. It's done."

"Good," Lola said. "I don't want Penny to ever want to see him. Is that clear? You must make sure of that."

"What is it you wish me to do?" Olive said.

Lola pursed her lips. "I want you to wear your most exciting dress—the one that seems to be painted to our hips. Then I want you to drink with him as much as possible."

Olive shook her head. "He won't drink with me. He would see through it. No there is only one way. I must go to his hotel room and lie there waiting for him."

"Wearing as little as possible," Lola said laughing. She got up and picked up some bottles of perfume. "Take these and rub them carefully on your bare skin. All over. I don't want you to smell like any of the girls on the line. I want him to go a little loco when he sees you. You'll drive him wild lying nude on his bed with this stuff on you."

"Si, si," Olive said grinning at the idea.

"I don't have to tell you what to do once you have him ready. Even though you do not like him, you must make love to him passionately as you can Olive. Can you remember that. He must want you again and again. I want you to sleep overnight there if possible."

Olive grimaced. "I hate the idea of offering myself to him again. After the way he acted before. But for you okay. I will love him in a way that he will never forget. He will know he has been truly with a woman. I will drive him out of his senses. I know how."

"Tell me how," Lola said matter-of-factly.

Olive described her caresses and embraces and her technique so vividly that Lola blushed slightly, a thing she did not ordinarily do.

"If he does not fall for all that," she said. "He must be made of iron. Now I will explain how you can get into his room dear!"

CHAPTER NINE

The next afternoon Johnny Blaise almost danced down the wooden platforms on Front Street as he hurried toward his hotel. Penny had promised to come to his room to sew his shirts as soon as she was through with school. Afterwards they would have dinner at one of the newer places in town.

He felt enormously elated. Nothing could deflate his joy. Not even Lola's insistence that Penny hold him off for a week. He would wait a month if need be. She was worth it. Meanwhile he was busy getting some new clothes made from the best tailor in town, talking to cattle dealers and persuading Jake and the other boys not to leave town too quick. Penny had expressed a desire for a big church wedding when she married and he wanted the hall filled.

It took a lot of maneuvering to block Jake Harkins' attempts to get him back to the cribs and the dance halls. Without telling Jake exactly what was happening, he explained he was too tired to do any more wenching for a while. At the same time he stayed away from the bottle. Penny did not like drunks.

As he entered Greene's hotel he glanced at the clock on the wall. He had ten minutes to get washed and put on a fresh shirt before she came. He bounded up the stairs, two at a time and whistled a favorite trail tune as he strode down the hall. Automatically he put his key in the lock and swung open the door. What he saw almost paralyzed him. There lying on his bed in nothing but a pair of frilly undershorts or whatever they called women's underpants was Buck Ranston's dance hall girl, Olive Gomez. Dozing peacefully.

For a moment he thought he had blundered into the wrong room. Buck Ranston lived down the hall. Then he saw his things around the room and knew it was his. There was only one conclusion to draw. Little Olive was in the wrong bed.

"Honey," he said nervously. "I hate to wake you up. But you're in the wrong room. Buck's is down the hall. No. 28."

The beautiful Mexican girl opened her eyes and smiled at him. "I know that Senor Blaise." She reached for a half-filled bottle nearby.

"Well then get over there please," Johnny pleaded. "I don't think he'll like it if he catches you here."

Olive smiled playfully and raised one of her well-shaped legs. "I'm not in the wrong room darling. I'm in the right one. You hurt my feelings by betting on that blonde tramp the other day. I want to prove to you my beauty is twice as lovely as hers."

Rising lazily from the bed, Olive loosened her underpants and stepped out of them, stark naked. He turned his back on her and began to go through his clothes in the closet. The sight of those globe-like breasts, those robust thighs was more than he could take now.

"Get dressed and get the hell out of here," he said. "If you're not gone in five minutes, I'll throw you out of that window."

He heard her laugh. "No you won't darling. What would everyone think. Especially Miss Flynn."

He voice was blurred as if she had been drinking heavily before he had come. She came up behind him as he bent over his things, swaying drunkenly and heavily against him, her breasts like hot hard cushions against his back. He stiffened as he felt her against him and her hands moving around his waist, creeping under his shirt and caressing the skin of his stomach. Fear of being trapped fought the swirling desire that surged through him.

"Don't be afraid," she whispered. "Buck doesn't care and he won't know. And if Miss Flynn comes, pretend you're asleep."

JOHN TANNER

"Please get out of here Olive," he said hoarsely. "Who the hell sent you up here, Buck or Jake?" It was the kind of crazy joke those varmints would play on a man in love and hoping to get through the next few days without raising hell. Both men knew he hadn't gone near any of the whores since Sherman's arrival.

She accepted his momentary stiffening as a signal that she could go ahead. Before the words had left his throat she moved in tightly against him so that he was aware of every full-fleshed curving part of her body. He could feel the heat of her right through his clothes. Her lushly rounded thighs moved against him and made perspiration break out on his temples. In spite of himself he began to react to her skilfull caresses. He did not want to, he wanted to get her out of there.

"Please get dressed Olive," he said, his mouth dry. He removed a five dollar bill from his jeans and held it out to her. "I know the boys meant well, but I gotta get you out of here pronto. I'm going to have a visitor soon."

She ignored the money and threw her arms about his neck. She kissed the side of his neck, then moved her lips to his ear. He shuddered as he felt her tongue, wet and fiery, dart into his ear.

"Get out of here Olive," he pleaded.

"No," she said laughing drunkenly. "Tell your visitor you're too sleepy." She began to play with his belt, to loosen it. He stared at her, almost hypnotized by what he saw in her face. Her eyes were as wild as an animal's. Her breathing was heavy as if she were in pain. Her firm, pointed breasts heaved tumultuously as she laughed, and the heat of the small, closed room made her flesh glisten with moisture.

He had to pull at his pants to keep her from tearing them away. "You're stinking drunk," he said, a little amused, despite his tension. He made one last effort. "Do me a big favor and go. I'll give you ten if you go Olive."

"You fool," she said. "I can teach you things about love little Penny never would dream of. Send her away."

He stared at her surprised. "How do you know she's coming here?"

She shrugged. "What difference does it make Chico. Take your things off and come to me. Don't answer when she comes. We can both ignore the little goose from Boston."

Something in her voice put him on guard. Was it that the blurredness was less or that the malice was more. At any rate, he swallowed and said in a firmer voice: "Get out."

"No, Chico," she said, as she lay naked on top of his coverlet. "You don't really want me to go."

A second later her eyes widened with terror as she found herself staring into the barrel of his gun.

"Get up!" he said brusquely. "I may be a stupid son of a gun but not that stupid. So you knew she was coming?"

"No, no," she said, crawling away from the gun as she felt its cold steel against her breast. "I just came to see you Johnny."

"I'll count to ten slowly," he said. "If you don't have all your duds on by then and one foot out of that door, you'll get a bullet between those pretty eyes. Now jump to it!"

There was no mistaking the seriousness of his tone. He meant business. With a leap that surprised him, she dived for the clothes she had piled on a chair beside the bed and began to dress with lightning-like haste.

Johnny watched her coldly. She was a beautiful animal, he thought. Built for love as a locomotive is built for pulling a train. As she moved quickly to get dressed, she looked more desirable than ever and he could understand Buck's interest in her. The taut firm flesh of her thighs and hips, the way her breasts rose and fell in rhythm with her accelerated breathing, the fear and anger in her dark eyes would make any man lose his grip, he thought, especially a man like Buck who had been on the lonely trail for weeks. As she bent over to button up her shoes, her eyes caught his and he saw the anger blazing in them. He would hate to have her come behind him in a dark alley, he thought.

Probably shove an Arkansas toothpick right in his back, one of those long thin knives that some of the dance hall girls carried to defend themselves against drunken bull whackers and freighters who beat them.

He finished his counting as he glanced out the window. Penny Flynn was coming up the boardwalk. His heart began pounding as he saw her approach the hotel entrance. He whirled around to face Olive. The Mexican girl was finishing buttoning up one of her shoes. As soon as she saw the look on his face, she jumped up and moved to the door.

"I'm going, I'm going," she cried terrified. "Don't shoot!" She nearly ripped the door off its hinges in her haste to open it.

Two minutes later, Penny Flynn knocked on his door. He took a deep breath and then opened it slowly. For a horrible moment he feared that Olive Gomez had returned for something she had forgotten. When he saw Penny's smiling face, he felt as if a stone had been lifted from his shoulders. He ushered her into his room with alacrity and closed the door.

"Let's leave it half open," she said awkwardly. "I'm not stuffy or anything and I trust you, but I am a schoolmarm and you know how respectable women are. I don't want any gossip about us."

"Anything you say honey," he said taking her hands and kissing them.

"I saw one of Lola's girls running out of the hotel as I came in. She almost knocked me down and when I tried to apologize, she sailed right past me with the angriest look I ever saw. I wonder where on earth she was rushing to like that. I've never seen her move that fast at the Golden Burro."

At that moment Olive Gomez was rushing to Lola's office in the Golden Burro. As soon as she closed the office door behind her, a tirade of abuse spewed from her lips.

"All right, all right," Lola said impatiently. "I know how you feel about Blaise. What happened?"

"Nothing happened," the Mexican girl said shrilly. "He threatened to blow my head off with his gun."

"He didn't make love to you?" she asked surprised.

Olive shook her head.

Lola banged the table with her fist. "You little fool, you didn't do what I told you. I told you to take your clothes off and get into his bed."

"But I did!" Olive shouted. "I did."

"And you tried to get him excited?" Lola asked.

Olive nodded. "It was no good. At first he seemed to want me and then he changed his mind. I don't know why."

"Oh never mind," Lola said. "Go on downstairs. I've got to think things over."

An hour later she called another girl into her office, a big, beautiful blonde from New Orleans whose snow-white bosom could be seen almost entirely in the extremely low cut dress she wore. Carefully she explained to the girl what she must do, how to enter his room when Greene was absent and how to trap Blaise. The girl nodded.

An hour later she was back. Greene had been there all the time. When she told him Johnny had asked her to wait in his room, he shook his head adamantly.

Lola's heart sank as she heard the girl's report. She mulled the girl's words carefully and finally came to a difficult decision.

The Mexican girl had put Blaise on his guard. He would be suspicious of any woman who approached him now. Any woman that is except herself.

She smiled inwardly as she thought of what she planned to do. In all the years she had been on her own, she had never seen any man who could turn her down. She did not offer herself to anyone now. Let the bastards buy her liquor and lose their hard earned money in her card tables, but they couldn't buy her. Every night when she came down those stairs, she saw dozens of eyes eye her hungrily. Some of the heaviest players had tried to make her break her rule that she never went up to bed with any gambler. It was not because she was a prude. Far from it. If she liked a man enough she would not let any house rule bother her. But she had never seen anyone yet who made her flesh crawl. Once before there had been such a man, but he had been killed. Since then there had been no one.

She kept her body to herself, but she knew that any man in her place would give a month's pay to know it better. She stood up now and eyed herself as she walked up and down in front of the long glass. She studied the swelling mounds of her breasts as she strutted before the mirror, the long shapely legs which were shown on the glass as she lifted her skirts to the knee and the movement of her sensuous hips.

"Yes Mr. Blaise I don't think you'll pass that up. And we'll see that little Penny gets an eyeful that she won't forget."

At that she was being extraordinarily good to him, she thought with satisfaction. She was giving him something she had kept from men a hundred times better than he. For a moment the thought of it annoyed her so much, she wanted to forget it. Then she shrugged. Sleeping with the cowboy would be no fun for her, but if she had to do it to save her sister from making a fool of herself, then she would do it ten times over.

A few minutes later she walked down the stairs. She was pleased to see the reaction of the gamblers. To a man they craned their heads to see her, pushing back the brims of their stetsons, putting down their cards and their drinks. She had no fears about Johnny Blaise. At the bar, she hailed Sam Billings and turned her head toward a quiet corner of the big hall. He followed her quickly and sat down beside her.

"I heard from Olive that it was no good," Billings said. "I think I'll handle this my own way."

"What's that?" Lola asked.

"I'll challenge him to a fight," Billings growled. "And if I kill the bastard that's it."

"And if you're killed instead?" she said scornfully. "Don't be a fool. The Texan's a good shot. As good as you are and maybe better. Besides if Penny finds out you're out to kill him you've completely lost her. I know my sister."

"Well what the hell do you expect me to do?" Billings said bitterly, "stand around and let him walk off with her. He won't go for any of the girls you send him. That's clear isn't it?"

"Except one."

"Who?" the big man asked.

"Me," Lola said grimly.

Billings looked impressed.

"You think it'll work?" he asked smiling.

"Yes, if we plan it carefully. Now listen carefully. This is what I want you to do. Make a note of the time and the signal. I'm going to take Penny to the dressmaker, Mrs. McSorley, tomorrow afternoon. The fitting will take a long time. It always does and she's making several things for her. Now I'm going to develop a sick headache after a while and leave for the hotel. You'll have to pick her up in a rig and bring her into town. When you get there you'll know if I wave a handkerchief in the window that I'm in a very compromising situation."

"I look up at his window when I get back?" he said.

"My window." she said. "My room, as you know is next to her boyfriend."

He looked at her admiringly. "You should have been a lawyer Lola," he said. "You make Machiavelli sound like a Sunday school teacher."

She smiled pleased. "I'm going to write down everything. It'll have to be timed carefully."

CHAPTER TEN

As he finished his lunch the next day, Johnny received a note from Lola Flynn. It was delivered to his table at the Western Hotel by one of Lola's girls. The note surprised and pleased him very much. It read:

Dear Mr. Blaise,

From what Penny tells me I may be your sister-in-law soon. I think we should know one another better. There is a great deal I would like to discuss with you since I am naturally concerned with my sister's happiness. I thought it would be nice if we three could dine together this evening. But first I would like to discuss some matters with you privately. I think it would be best if you could come to my room for a drink about four this afternoon. Penny will meet us there later and we will go out to dinner. I hope you are free.

cordially yours,
Lola Flynn

The girl who had brought the note said that Lola wished to know whether he could accept the invitation. Johnny nodded quickly.

Lola's friendly overture delighted him. He had been afraid she might influence Penny against him. Especially after his defeat of Anders' scheme against Sherman. The note indicated she was reconciled to the marriage. Naturally she would want to have a family talk with him. Penny was her only sister. Immediately after lunch he hurried to the barber shop for a close shave and a haircut. Then he bought Lola a beautiful comb as a gift. Once he was back in his room, the meeting began to make him apprehensive. He relaxed by writing his brother Tom a long gossipy letter about the adventures on the trail and in Dodge. To his surprise he was able to write several pages about Penny and his hopes of marrying her. He even wrote that they might not get to Texas till late because Penny might want to go back to Boston to see her aunts.

"I wish I could tell you what she's like Tom," he wrote. "I get weak in the knees when she comes close. She's got a beautiful sister, too. Lola. I thought she hated my guts for saving Sherman's hide, but she's invited me to dinner tonight."

He posted the letter and came back. It was only three o'clock and he decided he needed a drink. He opened a bottle of Texas Tanglefoot and took a couple of hearty swigs. A couple of more a little later settled the butterflies in his stomach. He was ready for the Big Sister private talk, and had mustered all his facts about how he and Penny would live on the ranch etc.

Promptly at four he went to Lola's room. He was dressed in his best clothes and carried her gift in a neat package.

If he was nervous when he arrived, Lola soon put him at his ease. She welcomed him warmly and asked him to relax in one of the easy chairs in the living room. He was impressed with the layout. There were two rooms, Lola explained, a bedroom and a parlor. The latter was furnished with a beautiful carpet Lola had sent from St. Louis, some fine upholstered chairs, a French refectory table and some exquisitely wrought lamps. There was a cabinet of dark wood which opened to reveal a magnificent array of bottles and glasses and a couch which she said was French Empire in style.

Lola herself was dressed in a beautiful yellow crinoline gown with white frills. It had a very low neckline which showed the tops of her full bosom to great advantage and made him a little queazy because he did not want to stare at them. To make sure that his behavior was proper he kept his eyes on her lovely red hair and face, as she sat on the couch opposite him.

She was delighted with her gift and told him so. "Please relax Mr. Blaise. Light up a cheroot if you want to. They don't bother me. I'll make us a drink. Would you rather have whiskey or brandy? I have some good cognac if you like such things."

Johnny hesitated. He wanted to make as good an impression as he could.

"I'd like to have some cognac," he said politely.

She poured him a full glass of it which he proceeded to drink in deep swigs as he did whiskey. He decided he did not like it as much as whiskey but did not say anything. He accepted another glass with a smile and began to drink it. It was not till he had put down half of the second drink that he realized how potent the stuff was.

"Now please tell me about yourself Mr. Blaise," she said. She smiled shyly. "May I call you Johnny?"

He nodded pleased. After that they were on a first name basis. Afterwards Johnny could not remember exactly when he went to sit beside her on the couch. It must have been after the drunk had made him a little unsteady on his feet. When he brought her another drink, and she patted the couch next to her, he thought it a good idea, and moved beside her.

Lola sighed inwardly with relief when he moved to the couch. She had feared he would sit opposite her all the time. It would be too difficult to do anything that way.

As soon as he was on the couch beside her, she could go to work. She arranged her dress so that he could see nearly all of her breasts when he looked at her. A moment later she saw that he had seen them by the flush that spread over his face.

"You're a very handsome young man," she said thickening her voice to match his own blurred tone. "I was afraid you would not like me."

"Hell, no," he said, "how could you think that? I like you very much. I think you're wonderful to invite me here like this."

"Let's drink a toast to a long friendship," she said smiling. She poured him another glass of brandy and sipped the same sherry she had poured herself earlier. He drank it quickly as he had the other cognac. He began to laugh suddenly with relief.

"You know, Lola, I was really scared of you. No fooling. I was afraid even to come in to talk to you." He laughed drunkenly.

"That's crazy," she said. "I liked you from the first. I'll prove it." She leaned forward, took his head in her hands and kissed him on the lips. He responded warmly, then pulled away a little when her tongue darted into his mouth. She loosened her dress so that one rounded breast was almost completely exposed. He stared at it drunkenly but something seemed to hold him back. She kissed him again and this time he stayed with her longer and clung drunkenly to her lips. Her heavy perfume was making him dizzy.

She tried desperately to arouse him. The time was getting short and Billings would be there soon for the signal that would tell him he must get Penny immediately to the hotel. But before she could give him the signal, she had to get him to remove all his clothes and go to bed. So far he showed no inclination to make love to her. He had kissed her but only because she kissed him first.

She sought desperately to arouse some desire in him. At one point she even lay back and let him stare at her legs, rolling back her skirts as if she were too drunk to care about anything. She took care that her garters could be seen by him.

She saw him examine her exposed form with surprise, but he did not make any advances. Finally, throwing caution to the winds, she made the advance herself. What difference did it make? He was too drunk to know what was happening anyway. It was simply that some inner control was preventing him from seizing her as any other man would after being given so much provocation. Aside from stripping completely and inviting him to make love to her, she had given him enough hints to do anything he wanted, here or in the bedroom inside.

She moved closer to him and kissed him again.

"I guess we're both drunk she said laughing. "But it doesn't matter. You might say it's in the family."

She bent over him and brushed his face with her lips, pressing her firm breasts against him. Her hands began to caress his face and neck and she crushed her body against his.

It was to no avail. She could tell he was reacting to her like a man aroused. Everything about him proved it, but he would not make the advance she hoped for She had been so sure that it would be so easy that she had not been at all concerned. How could anyone simply continue to sit beside her after those kisses, after those caresses, after the sight of her disarranged dress and her semi-nudity?

It was uncanny, but although he was obviously aroused, he would not seize her in his arms. There was only one thing to do and not much time left to do it in. She must get him drunk enough so she could undress him herself and put him in her bed.

She gave him more cognac and watched him drink it with a glassy look in his eyes. Yet even then, something inside made him hold back instead of taking her as any other man would have. He pulled away from her at one point and shook his head.

"I'm sorry, Lola," he said in a thick voice. "I guess that French stuff kicked me like a mule. I can't even see straight."

"Let's drink a toast to yours and Penny's happiness," she said, filling his glass again. She put her glass to her lips.

He drank another glass of the brandy although he did not want any more. A moment later she proposed another toast and again he drank reluctantly. After that he dozed off and fell back against the couch.

Quickly Lola lifted him and walked him into the bedroom. She lay him down on the bed and let him sleep a few minutes. Then she pulled off his boots and removed his clothing. He opened his eyes groggily from time to time as she continued to undress him, but he could not quite make out what was happening.

At one point he said, "Don't want Penny to see me drunk."

"Don't worry, dear," Lola said. "You'll be all right when she comes. Just sleep a few minutes."

In another moment, she had all his clothes off. He smiled foolishly at her several times. When his eyes were closed again, she began to strip. A few moments later she went to the window in her robe and looked down. As soon as she caught sight of Billings, she waved her handkerchief. He nodded when he saw her and immediately walked off.

Afterwards there was nothing to do but wait. She removed her robe and got into bed beside him. She had no trouble with him. He was fast asleep. For some reason, his sleeping so soundly irked her all the more. She had been so sure he would try to make violent love to her once she had given him an opening. Instead the fool had refused to take the bait and had fallen asleep. He had her completely stripped and in bed with him, something none of the men in Dodge could achieve, and he was fast asleep!

She began to talk to him at intervals but he heard nothing.

Twenty minutes later she heard a sharp knock on the door that led to Penny's room. She shut her eyes and waited for Penny to come in.

A moment later the door opened and Penny entered.

"Lola I was sure you were in ..."

She stopped suddenly and stared horrifiedly at the man in bed with her sister. For a second she stood there stunned. Then she turned angrily on her heel and went back to her room, slamming the door behind her. The sound woke Johnny. He sat up in bed, his eyes blinking and looking about him. When he saw the nude girl beside him, he paled and then got out of bed quickly. He stared at her unbelievingly. She seemed to be sleeping peacefully.

Through the door he heard Penny tell Billings in a high pitched angry voice:

"Is that why you didn't want me to go in there? You knew he was there all the time?"

"I'm sorry Penny," Billings said. "I had an idea this might be happening. Lola told me he had insisted on having a private talk with her here. But I didn't want you to see it."

"Take me away from here," she said sobbing.

Johnny hunted desperately for something to cover his nakedness. He had to stop her somehow. The only thing he could find was Lola's robe. Still groggy he put his arms into the loose robe and tied it around him. Then he moved quickly to open the door.

"Penny," he said, as he swung it open. "Wait. Let me explain."

She stared at him with mouth agape. Then rage overwhelmed her.

She began to throw everything she could get her hands on at him. He was so stunned he made no attempt to defend himself. A moment later he collapsed to the floor as a heavy porcelain bowl struck his head.

When he regained consciousness later he found himself lying on his own bed. Apparently Billings had carried him there. His head ached terribly, and for several moments he could not remember anything. Then, suddenly everything came back to him and he winced.

He had to find Penny and explain somehow so that she would understand. He went to her room, but she was not there. As fast as his legs could carry him, he raced to the Golden Burro. The bartender threw him a hostile look.

"Where's Miss Flynn," he asked quickly. "I've got to see her."

"She don't want to see you cowboy," the bartender growled. "I've got instructions to bar you from the place. Now get going before I have to call the Marshall."

He was too intent on finding Lola and Penny to pay the man any heed. He mounted the stairs to Lola's office and pushed open the door. She was sitting at her desk. When she saw him, she looked pained.

"Look, I gave instructions to keep you out," she said acidly. "How did you get up here?"

"Lola, I'm sorry, I got drunk and passed out on your bed," he said. "But you've got to explain what happened to Penny. I've got to explain to her. Where is she?"

"She doesn't want to see you," Lola said coldly. "She doesn't hold with cowboys who try to seduce her sister. If I were you I'd leave town."

"Seduce you?" Johnny said incredulously. "You must be out of your mind. You invited me up there and gave so much of that French brandy my back teeth were floating. All I did was pass out. Hell, you were pretty drunk yourself Lola, don't you remember that?"

"No," she said brusquely. "You got drunk and tried to rip my dress off. Luckily you were too far gone to do anything but pass out."

"You know that's not true Lola," he said pleadingly. "Look let me see your sister. I can make her understand."

"Penny doesn't want to see you," Lola said angrily, "can't you get that through your fool skull."

"But Lola," he pleaded, "you know I didn't do …" He stopped as he saw the look on her face, and remembered something.

"You arranged the whole thing," he said grimly. "You framed me so Penny wouldn't marry me. You put yourself in bed with me so she'd catch us there," he told her angrily.

She laughed. "Goodbye Cowboy. And don't drop in next time you're in town."

He had no idea where he went afterwards, only that he drank until he could not stand up. Ultimately Jake Harkins caught up with him and took him home.

The next day he tried in vain to see Penny. She refused to talk to him. She sent back his notes of explanation unopened, unread.

He went on the biggest drinking spree of his life then, covering every honky-tonk on Front Street that he could stand up in. When he could barely stand he headed for the line of cribs with Buck and Jake, and several other cowboys.

"Let's go see Frenchy," Jake said. "Okay Johnny, or are you still swearing off women?"

"Hell no," Johnny said. "The more the merrier. Let's go to Frenchy's She's a whore, but she's the only woman in this son-of-a-bitch town with a heart."

He never made it. He was sick just before he reached her shack and when she saw him he had passed out completely.

CHAPTER ELEVEN

A t the first slowing of the train the tall man opened his eyes. He was riding backwards, his boots on the green plush seat opposite him, facing the rest of the wooden coach. He pushed the flat-crown white Stetson higher so he could see the dusty Dodge City platform as the locomotive made its last shrill whistle. Then the train stopped suddenly. For a moment he sat there looking at the cowboys idly watching the train. The interest was mutual. The cowboys, dressed in dirty levis and open shirts, were obviously amused by the long-boned stranger with deep set dark eyes and aquiline nose who sat inside in a fancy black frock coat and Stetson. The amusement was tempered by respect when he stood up and they saw his cartridge belt and twin pearl-handled revolvers.

"Dodge City!" the conductor yelled as he moved quickly through the coach. "End of the track!"

The tall man saw the conductor swivel his head to look directly at him and met his eyes coldly. Hastily the trainman moved on down the aisle. The traveler waited for the last of the two men to go by him before moving away from his seat. One or two of the hurrying men stared at him as they moved ahead, but looked away quickly when his eyes rested on their faces. When the passengers had left the coach, he took down a heavy carpet bag from the overhead rack and headed for the exit.

The conductor tried to be friendly as he passed him again.

"Did you say you were staying in Dodge a while?"

"I didn't say," the traveler said, shortly.

"Well didn't mean to pry," the conductor said awkwardly. "Just thought I'd recommend a hotel if you were."

"Don't let it bother you," the traveler replied in his deep, polite voice. Then he smiled a little. "I'm not sure how long I'm staying."

"Well, anyhow, the Western Hotel's pretty good," the conductor said. The stranger's hardness made him uneasy.

The tall man stepped through the exit and jumped onto the dust below the coach. He peered through the crowd waiting for the train and then glanced at his gold turnip watch. After waiting a moment, he turned to a group of young women standing nearby.

"Excuse me ma'am? Could one of you kindly direct me to the Western Hotel?"

A tall, strikingly pretty red-haired girl studied his face curiously and smiled. He smiled back.

"It's just down about a hundred and fifty yards to the left," she said.

"Thank you ma'am," he said in a pleasant bass tone.

The red-haired girl smiled again.

"Staying in town long?" she asked.

"That could be," he said. "I don't know yet."

She nodded. "Well you're always welcome over at the Golden Burro. Down by the river."

"Thank you ma'am," he said smiling again. "I'll remember that. What do they call you ma'am if I'm not being too bold?"

"Lola," she said, grinning in a friendly way. "And you?"

"Tom," he said. "Well thanks again and I hope our paths cross."

He bowed, turned around and walked in big strides toward the Western Hotel. Lola watched him walk.

"Lola," Penny said, smiling at her sister's spellbound expression.

"You look as if someone had hit you between the eyes with an axe. Is he that fascinating? I didn't get a good look at him."

"Who said anything about his being fascinating," Lola said, blushing. "He just has an interesting face that's all. Good Lord can't I give directions to a man without being accused of turning to water?"

"No," Penny said smiling. "I didn't mean anything like that. It's just that I've never seen you look at a man like that before."

"Well that's all you see then. A look," Lola said tartly. "You won't catch me falling madly in love with some fool who comes in fresh out of town like you did with young Blaise. Look at him now. Filthy drunk twenty hours a day and spending every dollar he's made gambling. He's living on hand-outs from his friends and when they leave he'll be rolling in the street like a drunken Indian. Thank God I stopped you from marrying him."

Penny winced. "Please Lola, people are listening to you. Why do you keep bringing it up? I told you I made a bad mistake."

"Because I'm trying to show you how rare a man like Sam Billings is," Lola said. "He's told me he's going back to Chicago next week because you won't make up your mind."

Penny did not answer.

"Will you please give him an answer by Saturday," Lola said. "An intelligent answer. I promise you you won't get many chances like this. Don't throw it away Penny."

Penny sighed. "I guess you're right. I think I just had to have more time."

"It's been weeks since Blaise pulled that ..."

"Oh Lola please don't talk about it anymore!" Penny said, flushing darkly. "I'll talk to Sam tonight. Can we go now? I guess your new dress just hasn't come from New York yet. At least not today."

"Too bad," Lola said thoughtfully, looking at the direction the stranger had gone. "I would have loved to have worn it tonight."

As he reached the entrance of the Western Hotel, the tall man heard his name called by a familiar frog-throated voice. He turned to see Jake Harkins' huge bulk waddling toward him. Jake waited till he caught his breath, then mopped his brow with a red kerchief.

"I'm sorry I missed the train Tom," he said, shaking the visitor's hand. He snickered and winked. "I was up a little late with a lady from Omaha."

"You mean she just kicked you out of bed Jake?" Tom said good-naturedly.

"Hell no," Jake said laughing. "Warn't no bed. We were hotting it up under a tent. Some widow on the way to Denver."

He stood back and looked admiringly at the newcomer.

"You shore make the rest of us look like lice Tom. Anyone can tell you was educated to be a lawyer. Even when you're out with a herd you look ready to run for Congress."

"Come to the point Jake," Tom said. "Why didn't Johnny come to meet me."

Jake coughed and looked embarrassed. "Well, Tom, you see..."

Tom Blaise sighed and bit the end of a cheroot he took from his coat.

"That bad eh? Is he ever sober? Tell me the truth."

Jake shrugged. "Not often. Not since that business happened. He's kind of sick too Tom. Don't eat right. Practically drinks all his meals and don't even come in for cover when it rains. That's what's wrong with him now. He fell asleep in the open a week ago when we had an all-day rain and when they got him back to Frenchy's ... Well he's got a touch of fever. That's why Frenchy didn't come down. She was going to meet the train too."

"How soon can we get out to Frenchy's," Tom said grimly.

"We can make it in fifteen minutes. I got a rig waiting. Want me to bring it around or give you a chance to rest a little?"

"Bring it now Jake. I'll just give my gear to the hotel man. I want to see Johnny right away," Tom said in a tight-lipped voice.

When he saw his brother twenty minutes later, he was badly shocked. Johnny had lost a lot of weight, his face had a gaunt, unhealthy look and the straggly beard he had allowed to grow for weeks, made him look worse. He was delirious. Tom bent over him.

"Johnny," he whispered gently, "it's me Tom. I'm here to take you home."

"He doesn't hear anyone," Frenchy said sadly. "All he does is talk about her."

"Swear to God," Johnny was mumbling, "Swear to God I didn't touch Lola. Didn't do anything. Penny! Penny!"

Tom could not understand the rest of what he said. He tried to talk to Johnny. It was no use. At times the younger man would stop his ravings and stare at him. But all he said was:

"Tom," in a hoarse voice. "I swear I didn't touch her. I swear it."

When the doctor came to see him an hour later, Frenchy took Tom and Jake into the kitchen for some coffee. Tom came to the point at once.

"Tell me everything Frenchy. Your letter was kind of short. All you said actually was that Johnny was sick and broke and unable to come home."

Frenchy looked at her hands for a moment then told him what was common knowledge around town. That Johnny had been more or less engaged to Penny Flynn. That he had got her sister Lola very drunk and put her to bed a few days before he was expecting to get married.

"I just can't believe Johnny would do anything like that," Tom said stubbornly. "Sure he likes a good time. But he wouldn't pull this thing if he was in love with the girl and getting married—and I know he was. He wrote me a long letter about it. Well it doesn't make sense, Frenchy!"

"He was framed." Jake Harkins said angrily. "I've heard gossip in some of the saloons about it and Buck Ranston's girl, who works for Lola, as much as admitted it one day. But no one can prove it."

"I've heard Johnny say that too in his fever," Frenchy said. "Lola invited him to her place and got him drunk. But it's a drunken cowboy's word against a big dance hall owner. Once I even went to her to beg her to tell the truth and she laughed."

Tom Blaise stoop up. He was white-lipped with anger. He slapped his gun holsters. "I'm leaving," he announced suddenly.

"What are you going to do?" she said apprehensively.

"I'm going to make her tell the truth," he said angrily.

"I'd be a little careful Tom," Jake said. "She's got a couple of gunmen around to sort of watch the place. They'd shoot you if she blinked an eye. Let me and Buck come with you Tom?"

"No," Tom said coldly. "If there's any shooting I can take care of myself. But I'm not going to do any gunning. I'm going to try something I heard they did in a Mexican town once with a girl that told lies about people. Tell me all about the Burro and what goes on there, Jake. I've already met the lady."

When Jake had finished his report, the bull whacker added: "I'd better tell you that Bat Masterson is liable to make trouble if you start anything Tom."

Tom Blaise's eyes widened. "Bat Masterson is Marshall here? I thought he was in Wichita." He slapped his thigh and roared. "That really ties it Jake. Don't worry about Bat. Bat was with me in Mexico when we saw this little stunt. I'm sure I can handle him. Fact I think I'll stop over to his place right now. Hell's bells! He might decide to run me out of town if I don't. That would be a hell of an unfriendly thing to do. You come to the hotel in an hour Jake."

When he had left Johnny opened his eyes. "Was that Tom?" he asked. "I thought it was him."

"That was him," Frenchy said, kissing his hot brow.

"Damn it Jake," Johnny groaned. "Go out and stop him. If he loses his temper, he's liable to burn the whole damn town down. You know how he is."

CHAPTER TWELVE

The poker and faro tables were full when Tom Blaise entered the Golden Burro that night. The pianoplayer was playing a song that Lotta Crabtree had made popular the year before and the smoke hung over gamblers like rain-clouds. As he passed through the hall to the bar, Tom heard the clatter of dice in chuck-a-luck boxes, the click of ivory roulette balls—an innovation Lola had just put in, and the clink of silver. Moving past the crowd of raucous men laughing and joking at the bar were numerous dance hall girls in abbreviated costumes.

It hasn't changed at all, Tom thought as he moved up to the long bar. When he had first seen Dodge seven years ago it had tried to live up to its reputation as the wildest cow town of the West. He had liked coming up then, just as he had liked going to Abilene and Wichita. Then he had gotten tired of it. He preferred to do his gambling, drinking and wenching in Mexico. It was nearer and he found Mexican women more interesting than the blowsy farm girls who kept the liquor flowing in so many of the Kansas saloons.

If Johnny had not got into trouble, he might not have come back for years. He had his hands full with his breeding experiments on the ranch and he would be campaigning for Congress soon. To hell with Dodge and its whores. He could turn his back on them and not miss them in a hundred years.

But he could not turn his back on Johnny. The kid was an impulsive fool, granted, but he did not merit getting tricked by a saloon-owner who thought her kid sister was too good for him.

Aside from his lifelong hatred of such tactics there was the family honor involved. Maybe like so many Texans he was too damn touchy about it. Honor seemed to be a word that had disappeared from the dictionary. Even the deals he ran into among cattlemen sometimes made him sick. No matter. He took it seriously. Every Texas wrangler, cowboy and bull whacker who came within a hundred miles of the ranch would know the story soon. The Blaise name would be the butt of cheap jokes in bars from Dodge to Virginia City, unless he got even with her.

If the culprit had been a man he would have insisted that Johnny shoot it out with him. For that matter he would have been glad to do it himself. But how the hell could you shoot a woman? No, his way was better, he thought, smiling to himself.

"Something funny?" a man drinking a schooner of beer asked him.

"No," Tom said gruffly, "and what the hell is it to you?"

"Nothing," the beer-drinker said hastily, moving several feet away.

Tom felt foolish and almost told the man to have a drink on him. His temper was something he had always found hard to control. Especially if he thought anyone was too nosy. Where he came from it was considered a hostile remark to even demand a stranger's full name. You asked him his first name and that was it. His family name was his own business, unless he volunteered it.

"Well I'm delighted you accepted my invitation so soon," he heard a familiar voice say behind him. He turned to see Lola Flynn, looking more beautiful than ever in a gown of red satin with a low neckline that showed much of her white, swelling bosoms.

"I came as soon as I could," he said, removing his hat. "Looks like I may be in Dodge a while longer than I thought and a man needs some amusement."

"Well said," she smiled. "How about a drink Tom?"

She told the bartender to serve them the best whiskey he had at a table away from the bar. Tom bowed gratefully and followed her. While he drank, she looked at him curiously. He was one of the tallest men she had seen in Dodge. He must weigh at least two hundred pounds, she thought, but most of it is in his shoulders and chest and it looks good on him. She was impressed by the way he dressed too. The well cut black frock coat, the fine linen frill-front shirt and the slickly polished boots indicated that he was no mere cowboy or mule skinner. More likely a big rancher of some kind. She was dying to ask him questions, but she knew better. You just didn't plunge into a man's personal history in Dodge.

After a second drink he smiled and said:

"Say I hate to curry favor here, but do you think you could use your influence to get me the first vacancy at one of the poker tables? I'd like to play a few hands."

She smiled approvingly. He was no fool. If he had any desire to go on to deeper things with her he was in no hurry. She wondered if he could tell how strongly he affected her, how her heart had leaped when she saw him again in the Burro. She wondered if there was some change in her voice or color that he could see. She hoped not.

"Well do you think you can help me?" he said gently.

"Of course," she said quickly. "Right away in fact. Come with me."

She led him past the long bar to the other end of the hall where the games were in progress under several lanterns. The men barely noticed her, so deeply engrossed were they in their cards or what the dealer was giving them. At one of the poker tables, she stopped and looked over the shoulder of a gaunt-faced man with a cavalry-man's moustache who had a dwindling pile of chips in front of him. When he threw in his cards disgustedly a moment later, she patted his shoulder and said sweetly:

"You've lost enough for one night Harry. Let some one else take your place. Your luck's bound to change tomorrow night."

Harry looked amazed. "You're sure of what you're saying Lola?" he said. "I never heard you ask anyone to stop losing before. You inherit some money from a rich uncle or something?"

The sally triggered a round of loud laughter around the table. Tom, laughed with everyone else as he sat down. He was amused most by Lola's face. She looked as if she had just sucked a lemon by mistake. Oddly enough it made her look more appealing, he thought. What a damned shame she had to be a bitch. When she looked mad like she did now, she seemed like a little girl.

"Thanks Lola," Tom said easily. "Let me buy you a drink later after I sweeten the kitty a little."

His words melted her anger immediately. She smiled warmly at him and forgave him instantly for joining in the general laughter.

"I'll be waiting," she said warmly.

The rest of the night he got down to poker. He liked to gamble and when he did it he didn't want to think about anything else. It was like loving a woman. When you were doing it you were crazy to think of anything else. Otherwise you did it badly. In this case the gambling worked in well with his plans, but he made up his mind to forget Lola till it was time to stop playing.

He paid no attention either to the dance hall girls who were drawn to the tables like moths to a flame. The other men occasionally looked up as the prettier girls circled about them. Tom kept his eyes on his cards, or on the hands shown by the other players.

His strong back was such an obvious snub to the girls that Lola, watching from a few tables away, was amazed. Amazed and secretly pleased. The dealer at his table was nonplussed. Here was the greatest phalanx of womanflesh between Chicago and San Francisco, a choice that any man would have given his eyeteeth to have and the stranger wasn't even looking. As for Olive and the other girls who came near the table, if Lola had not been there, they would have turned and walked off. Even a dance hall girl wanted a man to notice she had a bosom and a figure.

The stranger played a hard game. He called every raise, no matter how high. Not a quiver of emotion played on his features whether he won or lost. His gaze was so formidable that none of the players could endure it for too long. If a player glanced at Tom's face, he looked away almost immediately.

After a couple of hours of playing the newcomer had amassed a pile of chips that drew awed glances from surrounding tables. The man's winning streak was absolutely uncanny. The dealer had not seen anything like it in months. From time to time he stole an apprehensive glance toward Lola. Finally, prompted by an impatient nod from the owner, he stopped dealing cards and leaned across to the stranger. It was not two o'clock yet but something had to be done to end his meteor-like streak.

As Eddie whispered into his ear, Tom looked up and appeared to have noticed the existence of the girls for the first time that night. Slowly his eyes canvassed the line of females, hovering carefully over their semi-exposed bosoms and the curves of their hips. Then his eyes moved about the room. He nodded toward Lola Flynn.

There was a hush and the dealer, always the diplomat, smiled. "Sorry mister," he whispered, "that's the owner of the Burro. She ain't in the running. Take my advice and pick the Viennese girl. She's out of this world."

Tom smiled wanly and shook his head. He appeared to have forgotten the girls as he continued to play. On the next seven hands, he picked up such an amazing sum of money that the players at the other tables stopped to watch. The stranger's phenomenal luck drew every eye in the house including Sam Billings who had come in late. As he raked in the big pots everyone followed his hand with a hypnotic stare. Lola grew more and more nervous as the dealer doled out expensive chips, in growing numbers.

After a while she disappeared from the gambling room. She came back ten minutes later with a mean looking, thinlipped man in a dark hat.

"That's Buck Lewis," his neighbor whispered to Tom. "One of the smartest poker players between here and San Francisco. He's supposed to be a silent partner in the Burro."

Tom said nothing.

Lewis sat in on the game and before anyone could say Wounded Knee. Wyoming, the tide had turned. Lewis was getting nearly every pot and they were big ones. It was beginning to look as if the stranger's immense winnings would be completely drained when he did something that startled them all. Right after Buck Lewis had won a pot of over 2,000 dollars, Tom grabbed his coat and shook it ferociously. Two aces fell out. No one was sure what happened next except that the red-faced cheat found himself on the floor with a shiner. When the fallen man suddenly pulled a gun, Tom shot it out of his hand.

And that was all. Cheating was cheating and if you caught some one doing it redhanded, you had the right to kill him. Everyone thought it was very merciful of the stranger to let Lewis go with nothing more than a black eye.

Everyone, that is, except Lola, who was losing an enormous amount as the stranger continued to rake in big pots. It was impossible to beat him because he was ready to bluff down to his last chip to drive the other players out. There was no way of telling whether he had a full house or a pair of fours. Lola begged Sam Billings to sit in on the game. But after a few hands even the burly Chicagoan had no stomach for such losses.

The game continued to go on. The Golden Burro's popularity with gamblers rested partly on the owner's boast that the sky was the limit and that no game was halted unless a player wanted time out. But something had to be done to stop the stranger soon or Lola knew she would be wiped out. Yet it might be as disastrous for her if he were to walk out completely now and go home. Then there would be no chance of winning back the enormous amount of money he already had won. She felt a faint ray of hope a little later when he began to yawn and take a longer time to study his cards. But when he began to talk about cashing in his chips soon and going back to his hotel, she became alarmed. Now that he was getting sleepy and had drunk several whiskies, he was likelier to slip and leave unnoticed certain of the dealer's tricks with the deck. But he seemed determined to go. It was then that Lola decided to break sharply with tradition. She whispered in the dealer's ear, nearly causing him to fall from his chair.

She offered herself to Tom.

When the dealer looked at her again as if he couldn't believe his ears, she nodded firmly.

Without another word, the dealer spoke into Tom's ear and saw him smile. He stopped playing long enough to run his fingers down her dress below the waist and then lifted her skirts to glance appreciatively at her legs. Lola colored at this liberty which drew snickers from everyone except Billings. But Lola did not flinch. She could not afford to. She had already lost $30,000.

"Would you like to go upstairs now please." she asked in a voice that controlled her fury.

"Wait a minute Lola," Billings said incredulously. "You can't do that. I won't let you."

"Please attend to your own business," she said white-lipped with anger. She turned again to the winner. "I'm ready mister."

Tom glanced idly at his gold watch and smiled.

"Well I was told you couldn't go upstairs till two o'clock. It's only one now. I think I'll play till then."

Lola colored, but there was nothing she could do. She had to sit by and watch him shovel in the chips again. Whether Buck Lewis' fate had made him cautious or Tom's cold stare had unnerved him, the dealer was reluctant to use any tricks. He was able to win a pot now and then by calling every one of the stranger's big raises, but in the end Tom came out ahead. By two o'clock he not only owned $30,000, some of it in Lola's notes, but most of the furnishings in the Burro.

Promptly at two o'clock, he slapped the beautiful redhead's derriere and told her he'd like to go upstairs. Afterwards, if she liked, he would give her a chance to win some of her money back, he implied.

"Here's a stake to get you started with," he said casually, as he pushed over a thousand dollars worth of chips.

As he spoke his eyes surveyed Lola's ample bosom and creamy white shoulders. His frank, hungry look surprised everyone and enraged Lola. She could not bear to be appraised like horseflesh and usually slapped anyone who tried it. This time, however, she seemed to purr.

He slapped her backside good-naturedly now and began to march her out of the room.

"You can take a rest son," he said to the dealer. "I'll be a while. Then if you like we'll play till morning."

"Well, I'm damned," chortled Jake, who had been watching the proceedings with great glee, "I never thought I'd see the day what the high-nosed filly would get rode."

"Shut your ugly mouth, you lousy trail-leavings," snarled Sam Billings, who realized that his last chance at both Penny and the Golden Burro was walking up the gilded stairs with the tall Texan. "And keep it shut, or I'll put a stopper in you you'll never forget."

The saloon, which had been buzzing with the unexpected success of Tom, suddenly became quiet as a prairie night. Even the bartender grew silent, as Jake Harkins turned to the dark Easterner and said: "Mister, where I come from, if a man is having a little fun, it's his own business, and not that of some fancy-dressed tin horn from the big city. Now you just say you're sorry, nice-like, and old Jake'll forget the ideas he had about turning you inside out like a Texas Twister." With this sally, the crowd began to chuckle, but the laughs died in the throats of most of the men and women in the place, as Sam Billings, his face a swarthy mask of fury, shouted "Draw, you long-winded son-of-a-bitch, if you've got the guts." With this, big Jake whirled and clawed for leather, but too much booze, and too many years of trail driving had slowed his reflexes. He didn't even get his gun cleared of its holster, when Billing's iron roared twice, and Jake fell dead. "You all saw," Billings cried, "He started to draw on me first."

"That's true, you louse, but you goaded him into it," said one of the men at the poker table.

"Anyone else feel like taking his place?" sneered Billings. "All right, then, some of you take that outside and get it over to Boot Hill. There's going to be some real excitement around here soon, and I don't want any bodies in my way when I make my play with that lanky bastard that thinks he's such a poker player!"

CHAPTER THIRTEEN

If Lola had seemed cool downstairs, she seemed positively driven by a passionate longing for the tall gambler when they reached the privacy of her room. She did not draw back when, at the door, he seized her in his arms kissed her hungrily and possessively and plunged his hand into the neck of her dress.

Tom glanced appreciatively at Lola's office. Lola obviously liked to live well. Her room was a good replica of the finest salons in New Orleans. The red plush chairs settee were of prime quality and her frosted glass chandelier could have been made by a fine craftsman. He assayed with a practiced eye the expensive paintings on the wall and the exquisitely wrought music box in a corner. The woman had good taste and she was beautiful and quick. The kind of woman he would have liked ordinarily. What a pity she was what she was.

"You like my taste?" she asked politely.

He did not bother to reply. Instead he threw his arms around her and fastened his mouth on hers. When he let her go she smiled and then kissed him longingly.

"I'm glad you insisted on me," she said mischievously, "I admit I was furious with you at first. The idea of anyone treating Lola Flynn like a common whore. The last man who tried that ate bullets!"

She smiled in a feline manner that expressed her secret pleasure.

"Would you like a drink of something really special? I have an idea you'll be able to appreciate it. Not many people here do."

She poured him a stiff beaker of cognac. He took it smiling.

"Thanks," he said. "I didn't pick you for the type that tried to get men stoned on cognac. As it happens I like the stuff very much."

She looked at him sharply.

"Now take those things off," he said masterfully. "I'm getting impatient."

Without a word Lola loosened her dress and pulled it over her head. In a moment she had nothing on but a pair of long frilly white drawers. He nodded and she removed those as well.

"Now you take your things off," she said invitingly.

"Let me see if you live up to your promise first," he said. His dark eyes surveyed her nudity coolly. She walked around the room as if she were a model, moving with a well-timed strut that set her full firm breasts in motion. He followed her undulating curvacious hips and the well-sculpted halfmoons of her buttocks. She was a beautiful woman all right. As she moved around the room not an inch of flabbiness showed on her robust thighs or belly. She was a thoroughbred, he thought, a beauty that any red-blooded male would be fired by if he saw her like this. If he could see her as she was now, naked, carrying herself like a queen, the firm globes of her breasts facing him like unassailable bastions. The slim, exquisitely turned ankles, the thin girlish wrists.

Normally, he thought, I could completely lose track of time by loving a woman like this, by possessing all that beauty. He had had many beautiful women. In the United States as well as Mexico, but none with the incredible sensuality of this red-haired goddess. It was not simply the size and shape of her breasts, the curves of her hips, the fullness of her thighs, it was also the fire in her eye, the pride and defiance that shone there even now when another woman might have been humbled, by being treated as she was being treated.

She stopped finally and looked defiantly at him.

"Do I live up to my promise?" she challenged.

He nodded.

"You don't know how lucky you are. There are cattlemen in Dodge who would give $5,000 to to go to bed with me. I hope you're satisfied."

He replied with a glacial smile.

"Where is your bed Madame?" he said slowly.

She seemed to be puzzled by his attitude but she said nothing. She led him to a small alcove screened from the room by drapes and drew them aside. Beyond was a large four-poster bed with excellent scrollwork on its wood.

"All the way from New Orleans," she said proudly.

His amused stare began to disturb her. She waited self-consciously.

"Would you like me to help you Tom?" she asked gently.

He continued to stare coolly at her. Suddenly he barked: "Turn around!"

She pivoted, showing him her ivory-colored roundness. His continued silence was ominous.

"Tom," she said nervously, "what are you going to do?"

In reply, he kicked her bottom roughly with the heel of his heavy Texas boot and sent her sprawling on the bed. Before she could understand what was happening, he slapped her backside so hard that she yowled in pain. Ignoring her yelps, he continued to lambast her with his big hand, raising red welts in her flesh. Then suddenly, he stopped and drew away.

When she finally dared turn around, she saw him lighting a cigar a few feet away. When he had it lit, he turned toward the door. She stared at him transfixed and then leaped at him, grabbing his leg.

"Tom don't go. Please. Stay with me." Her voice quivered with emotion.

He kicked her away roughly.

"Stay with you? Hell I wouldn't make love to you if you were the last girl between here and San Antonio." His voice was heavy with contempt.

"What?" she said unbelievingly.

"You're nothing but a lousy whore. Much worse than any of the girls who work for you. At least they turn an honest trick on a mattress. They don't go around trying to destroy people by conniving and scheming. Why don't you just shoot men in the back?. It's easier and quicker."

"Who are you?" she said, her eyes widening. She looked nervously at the two guns he carried.

"I'm Tom Blaise," he said slowly, letting it sink in, "Johnny Blaise's brother."

"Johnny Blaise?" she repeated, white-faced.

"Johnny Blaise," he said, "the poor boob you framed so he wouldn't marry your snotty sister. Turning him into a drunk who gambles every cent he has, drinks every brand of rotgut you sell in this lousy town, sleeping stinking drunk in the rain wherever he falls."

She stared at him terrified and glued her eyes to his holsters. He caught her glance.

"Don't worry. I'm not going to kill you. You're not worth the bullet to blow you into hell. If Johnny had died, I'd have opened you with Bowie knife. You're lucky the doctor says he's going to be all right and I can take him home. All I want from you is one thing more, then I'm through."

Slowly the terror drained from her face and her features relaxed into a knowing smile. He was a man like other men after all. He wanted her.

"I'm ready," she said, gazing directly at him.

"You were saying a while ago that no man here had ever seen you in your birthday suit, that right?"

"That's right."

"Nobody ever even sneaked a look at that bosom while you were taking a bath?" he asked smiling. "Nobody tried to peek at those gorgeous legs of yours when you were changing?"

"No one," she said proudly. "I'd have shot any man who tried it."

"That's a shame then Lola," he said slowly. "Keeping all that loveliness from mankind. I'll bet after you do one of your dances in those short costumes, and kick up those pretty legs, those men down there are fit to be tied. I'll bet they'd give plenty to see what I'm looking at now."

"What are you trying to say," she said puzzled.

"Only that I think we'll give them a show. Give the whole town a show in fact, a show that'll make the Golden Burro known from here to Paris, France."

With that he whipped his gun from its holster and put the cold barrel against her bare skin.

"March honey! To the door."

"What are you going to do with me?" she asked, terrified.

"We're going to show the boys of Dodge just what they've been missing. You operate a gambling palace here don't you? Or did before I took it over. Well I say it's time for the dealer to show all her cards. Go on down those stairs or I'll make you look like a sieve."

"No you can't," she cried pleadingly. "I'll give you anything you want, but don't make me go down like that."

"Get going girl," he barked.

"Please Tom," she begged. "I'll do anything. I'll make up Johnny's losses."

"With what?" he said sarcastically, "As of now you own nothing but what you had on your back. I'll tell you what you can do. You can tell that sister of yours the truth, that you tricked my brother and when you got him drunk enough you stripped him and put him in your bed."

"No," she said. "I can't do that."

"Okay honey, the discussion's over then. The curtain goes up on the best show Dodge's ever seen. March!" He punctuated his order by jabbing the cold metal of his gun deep into the small of her back.

Throwing open the door, he led her down the carpeted stairs. She moved at a snail's pace at first, then as he jabbed his gun harder against her back, she moved faster.

When the men below saw the naked girl appear the silence was broken by a clatter of glasses dropping on the floor.

For a long moment, everyone stared at Lola as if he were paralyzed with shock. Even Billings looked as if his eyes would pop out of his head. Lola Flynn was standing a few feet away, stark naked!

Before they could recover their senses, Tom spoke in a loud firm voice, holding a gun in each hand.

"Take a good look gents. This is Lola Flynn, known otherwise as Lady Godiva of Dodge City."

As Billings' hand began to move, Tom said quickly. "I wouldn't friend or I'll kill you. And then maybe your lady friend. You can ask her."

"Don't Sam, Lola begged. "He means it. He's Johnny Blaise's brother." Her words produced consternation on many faces.

"That's right friend," Tom said coldly as he held his gun at Lola's back. "If you all keep calm like a good audience nothing will happen. I don't mean to harm the lady. Just to show her at her best. Fact is she's naked because she just lost the last hand of strip poker we played upstairs."

The remark produced howls of nervous laughter that relieved the tension in the room. Tom Blaise spoke to Lola.

"All right Lola move! We're going outside for some fresh air." He pushed her ahead of him, keeping an eye on the crowd as one gun was pressed to her flesh. "Just in case you lads are thinking of interfering, the gun tickling Lola is cocked and ready to go," Tom said.

No one interfered. Sam Billings put his hand to his holster but did not draw. Instead he turned on his heel when Tom and Lola were at the doorway and vanished in the other direction.

Outside, Lola shivered as the cool night air moved against her bare flesh. Suddenly she saw someone lead a donkey up to the hitchrail in front of the building.

"Here we are Lola," Tom said pleasantly. "What could be more appropriate than to seat the owner of the Burro on a real live burro."

He lifted her quickly in his strong arms and lowered her on to the donkey's back.

"Please Tom," she begged. "Don't do this to me. I'll never live it down. I'm sorry for what I did to your brother. But don't do this."

"You're a little late with that Lola," he said dryly. "Okay start moving. He mounted his horse and followed them slowly.

"Okay folks," he shouted behind him, "the show's on. You can come out."

The men began to pour out of the Golden Burro taking care to keep a respectable distance between themselves and the Texan with drawn guns. A few yards away as they turned into Front Street, Buck Ranston appeared on a horse with his gun aimed carefully at the crowd.

"Don't shoot unless someone interferes with the performance," Tom told Buck. "And I don't think they'll do anything that foolish."

As the procession moved down the main street, the saloons and hotels emptied and scores of people lined the streets. They stared fascinated at the beautiful girl on the donkey who was dressed in nothing but moonbeams and red hair.

"That's sure a beautiful woman," a man was heard saying aloud. A second later a woman slapped his face hard and pulled him away by the ear. Instantly the few respectable women who had emerged into the street in night clothes clapped hands on their men and led them away.

It did not noticeable diminish the crowd. As the naked girl moved along on the back of the ass, howls of derisive laughter followed her, including some from women who hated her guts. She winced as she heard it and tried to shield her breasts and intimate areas. She did not try to shield them long. A bark from Tom stopped that.

They had their first sign of trouble as they neared the Greene Hotel. Suddenly they heard Billings' voice call out from the darkness. "Don't move another foot, Blaise! I've got you covered with a rifle."

Tom stopped as the crowd drew back frightened and got out of the line of fire.

"That's Billings," Tom heard someone say. "He's drunk. Get back. He'll shoot wild for sure."

"Where's Bat Masterson?" a stout woman growled, as she descended from the hotel followed by three tousled-headed youngsters. "I told you to stay in bed!" she screamed. "Don't leave the hotel!"

"Lady," Buck Ranston said. "Get those kids off the street! There's a man with a gun out there."

"I knew we shouldn't have stopped in this horrible place," the woman growled. "We've been waiting for my husband to come from St. Louis for four days. Where's the marshall?" she repeated petulantly. "He ought to put a stop to this disgusting, sinful thing."

"I don't know ma'am," Ranston said patiently. "But please get those kids out of here." He turned to a nine year old who had moved into the street and was staring fascinatedly at the woman on the donkey."

"Richard," the boy's mother screamed. "Come back! Good Lord how can you men do that in a town where there are women and children. Close your eyes Richard."

Richard paid no heed to his mother and easily eluded her grasp.

"Blaise," Billings' voice yelled again, "I'm giving you two minutes to get away from that girl or I'll blow your head off."

"Who is he?" Tom asked Buck. "He sounds like a mean drunk."

"He's some Eastern lawyer who wanted to marry Lola's sister. Hates Johnny's guts. Probably helped Lola frame him."

Tom made a quick decision. "I'm going after him. Get the girl out of the way until I come back. This is one show no one's going to interfere with. It's for Johnny."

As he moved away from the donkey with the nude girl on it, a piercing scream filled the air. The crowd stared up at a window in the Greene Hotel where Penny Flynn was exposed.

"Lola!" she screamed. "Stop them," she yelled at the crowd.

No one moved. Tom walked slowly toward the other end of the street, keeping close to the doorway. Suddenly a dark figure moved out of the shadows. It was Billings with a rifle ready to fire. For a second both men seemed to be frozen in their tracks. Then both fired almost at once. Both bullets missed. Billings darted back into the shadows while Tom moved closer.

Several things happened at once. The nine-year old, who had been staring spellbound at the scene, darted out of his mother's reach again and sprinted down the street directly in front of Tom Blaise. Penny Flynn came flying out of the hotel doorway in her nightdress as the child's mother screamed. Billings emerged from the darkness and began firing with a six-shooter and was answered at once by Tom's guns. Neither man noticed the child's vulnerable position at first.

Suddenly everyone was electrified as Lola leaped from the donkey's back and sprinted toward the child. She grabbed him in her arms and moved as quickly as she could out of the line of fire.

"Don't shoot for God's sakes," she screamed. It was too late. Both men fired almost simultaneously and a bullet from Billings' gun struck her shoulder. The child, unscathed, was seized by his mother.

Billings had exhausted the bullets in the gun and darted back into the shadows. Tom turned toward Buck, yelled to him to get Lola a doctor and then ran, firing both guns at Billings.

He caught up with him a moment later in an alley. Billings, perspiring freely, stared white-faced at the barrels of Tom's smoking guns.

"Don't shoot," he pleaded. "I'll give you anything you want."

"I want just one thing," Tom said contemptuously. "Get back to Lola's sister and tell her the truth about my brother."

"The truth," Billings said bewilderedly. The closeness of Tom's guns to his temple made it hard for him to talk. He inhaled the acrid odor from their hot barrels.

"You and Lola framed him didn't you?" Tom barked. "Make up your mind. You go back and tell her the whole scheme or I'll put a bullet through those pig eyes of yours right now."

Billings winced. There was no mistaking Tom's seriousness. "Okay," he growled. "Okay. She's not worth dying for."

A few minutes later Tom led him into the room where Lola was. The red-head was lying in bed with her eyes closed as a doctor bent over her. Her sister was looking on, white-faced, her hands trembling as she held a glass of whiskey.

"Give her some more," the doctor said. He turned to Tom and his captive. "Haven't you done enough damn it. Get out of here. I got work to do."

"She's all right?" Tom asked politely.

"She's going to have a mighty sore shoulder and arm for a while," the doctor said. "But she'll be all right."

"Good," Tom said. "That gal has more guts than a regiment of soldiers. Running after that kid."

Turning to Penny he said grimly: "Ma'am will you come into the next room? Mr. Billings has a confession to make about my brother."

"I don't want to listen to it," Penny began angrily. "Can't you see my sister is———'"

Lola opened her eyes. "Listen to him Penny. I want you to."

She winced. "Give me that whiskey, and then go inside while the doctor probes. I don't want you to watch that."

Despite her protests, Penny finally agreed to follow them. Several moments later after Billings had completed his confession she stared miserably at Tom and then covered her face with her hands.

A moment later she took them away and said quietly: "I'd like to go and see Johnny as soon as Lola's all right." She paused and added: "if he still wants to see me."

"He wants to see you very much," Tom said. He turned to Billings. "You can go now. But you'd better not come near me while I'm in this town. I don't like your smell."

Billings stared angrily at him and turned to go. As he did he collided with Bat Masterson who was coming through the door.

"Where the devil have you been?" Billings said resentfully. "Hell broke loose and no one could find you."

Bat Masterson smiled apologetically. "Did I miss anything? I'm sorry. I just went out to visit a sick friend over at Frenchy's."

He winked carefully at Tom Blaise.

Billings snorted and headed for the door, his big face red with anger. "I thought a marshall was supposed to be around when trouble popped!"

"I was, Mr. Billings. Where are you headed for, by the way?"

"I'm going to my room," Billings retorted.

Bat smiled sadly. "I don't think you are. I'm putting you under arrest for terrorizing a crowd, wounding a woman and nearly killing a child."

The Chicagoan looked as if he would burst with sheer wrath. "If you saw that Marshall," he expostulated, "then you saw Blaise force Lola to parade around naked on the back of a mule at the point of a gun."

Masterson raised his eyebrows. "Really? I don't remember seeing anyone naked on the back of a donkey."

"Lot's of people saw it," Billings said in a towering rage.

"I didn't see it," Masterson snapped, stressing the first word.

"Well why don't you ask Lola?" Billings insisted as the doctor came in."

Masterson twirled his cane and looked at the medic.

"Okay to talk to the lady Doc?" he asked blandly.

"So long as it ain't too long," the doctor growled. "I don't want her subjected to a cross-examination. She's pretty worn out."

Bat Masterson walked into the next room followed by Billings, Penny and Tom Blaise. Lola looked at them questioningly.

"This gentleman," Bat said pointing to Billings, "accuses Mr. Blaise of forcing you to sit naked on the back of a donkey at the point of a gun. Is that true Lola? If it is I'll have to take action."

Lola looked deep into her sister's eyes. For a moment there was silence as the color deepened in the red-haired girl's cheeks. She turned away, unable to face her sister's look of accusation.

"It's not true Marshall," she said hoarsely. "No one forced me to do anything."

The only man in the room who looked more astonished than Sam Billings was Tom Blaise.

CHAPTER FOURTEEN

A few weeks later several passengers, one of them a girl with her arm in a red silk sling mounted the train leaving Dodge City. As they entered the coach the conductor recognized a man in the party.

"Well you did stay in Dodge City a while after all didn't you?" he said.

"Yes I did," Tom Blaise said. "Longer than I expected."

The conductor waved them to some empty green plush seats and took their tickets. As he did a boy rushed up with a package and handed it to Lola who took it clumsily with her good hand.

"What's all this for Richard?" Lola said surprised.

"Wedding present from my mama for saving my life," the boy said as if he had learned the words by rote.

Lola blushed. She looked embarrassedly at Penny and Johnny and then at Tom. She handed the gift back to the boy with a sigh.

"Your mother made a mistake Richard. It's my sister who got married yesterday, not me."

"Oh she told me to give it to you," the boy said bewildered. "Then you don't want it?"

Lola looked unhappy. "No I can't accept it. I'm not married. Tell you ma thanks anyway."

As the disappointed boy turned to go, Tom Blaise stopped him with his Texas boot.

"Whoa there, son. Give that back to the lady. She's getting married soon."

For a moment everyone seemed stunned by his remark. Johnny gaped at him. Then Lola's eyes widened and a delighted smile grew on her pretty face.

"You mean you're proposing to me, Tom Blaise?"

Tom shrugged. "Well, I can't just let you out in the street. You don't have any money and your sister's going to be a thousand miles away. Besides, you can't even hardly fry yourself an egg and side of bacon with your arm in a sling. Hell, I'm not that mean."

Lola kissed him impulsively. "That's not the only reason you're marrying me, I hope."

"Well, no," Tom said, beginning to smile at last. "I never did like to buy a cow or a pig in a poke without seeing it from all angles. Well, I feel the same way with a wife."

He gave the boy a silver dollar as Lola's face indicated she was going to unloose a flood of angry words.

"Better go, sonny," he whispered. "It won't be safe for menfolk around here in a minute."

END

www.ingramcontent.com/pod-product-compliance
Lightning Source LLC
Chambersburg PA
CBHW030130260626
47156CB00008B/2880